"This is unreal," she thought. "This real. It can't be. But it is. It is real. Angus," she said to herself. 'The co you are so like him. You are the son one else. Oh God! How long is the arm of coincidence? Of all the young farmers in Scotland it had to be you and of all the ranches in Texas you had to come to this one."

The rising sun tinged the banks of mist with gold and he loved her long and tenderly and then she rose and washed and dressed. They had furach and coffee.

They were camped on a hillside in a picturesque little glen. Just down below them in the village a train was waiting, it seemed impatiently, at the station.

"Let's part just here. I shall manage to find my way to the station. It is only a little way. I want to leave you where I will want to remember you - in the wild country."

"Are you sure?"

"Yes."

"All the best."

"And to you."

They kissed only briefly.

Before she boarded the train she looked up to the hillside. There was a golden eagle soaring in the blue sky, its wings tipped with light. He stood on a rock beside a pine tree - a lone Highlander. The sun behind him made a halo on his hair.

"That is how it should be," she thought.

Charlotte Benson's Highland Fling

Booklocker.com, Inc.
2004

Charlotte Benson's Highland Fling

JK Maclean

Chapter One

A whirlwind was passing through the trees down below the house. It sucked up the dust and the dry leaves and carried them in a narrow spiral above the treetops. It was a small whirlwind, of the harmless kind quite common at this time of year, but, later on, and much further to the north, these would develop into the dreaded twisters, which wreaked havoc with everything in their paths.

As she waited for her quest to arrive, Charlotte looked out over the dry and dusty landscape. It shimmered in the hot sun.

"I hope we get rain soon," she said to herself.

Here in the Texas Panhandle, ranch life could be harsh in the hot summer months. The sun was now in the west and beginning to cast long dusty shadows. Her eyes were drawn to the lone pine. It was just visible on the skyline. She thought fondly of Tom. She still missed him. There was no bitterness in her, but she still missed him. She always would.

She looked at her watch.

"They'll be here soon," she thought.

A cloud of dust appeared down the road, billowing behind a pickup driven at speed.

"That is Rhona. Only Rhona drives at that speed and, oh, I do wish she wouldn't," thought Charlotte, as she turned indoors to set out a tray.

Of late, in moments of solitude, she found herself wondering about her elder daughter. Running the ranch presented no problems at all for Rhona. Ranching was something to which she had been born. Rhona handled running the ranch with ease and competence. Rhona handled just about everything she tackled with ease and competence. There was about her a sense of determination and energy that was absent in Charlotte's other children. She could never quite work out where this energy and competence came from. Just now and then Charlotte wished she was perhaps just a little less competent. She was popular among the younger set with which she mixed, but so far there was no serious romance. The young men who dated her seemed to defer to her too much. They seemed to put her on a pedestal.

"That won't impress Rhona in any way," Charlotte would think. "She needs someone who is his own man. I think she frightens them off."

Rhona even found time to play a prominent part in the 4H movement. She was now County Chairman of this organisation for the young men and women who made their living off the land. It was she who had been responsible for arranging the visit of the Scottish Young Farmers. A group of ten young farmers from Scotland had arrived in Dallas the previous night. They were to spend a week in San Miguel County as guests of ranchers. Charlotte was now awaiting the guest allocated to her. He was to stay with them for the week. There were many events arranged for the visit, which was to end with the San Miguel Rodeo. Ah! What happy memories that first rodeo held for her. That was the day the boys first saw the Bar C Ranch. The name had long ago been changed to the Lone Pine Ranch.

She heard the pickup come to a halt with a screech of brakes and then Rhona's voice rang out from the verandah.

"Mom," she called. "We're home. Come and meet Angus."

He stood on the edge of the verandah. She could see only the silhouette of a big man in a kilt. The westering sun behind him formed a halo around his hair.

"Mom, are you all right?"

"Yes. Yes, I'm all right. Why?"

"It's just ... oh, nothing."

"Yes, I'm just fine."

Angus came forward now. His hair was not the burnished auburn she had thought it to be. That was a trick of the light. She could look at him now without the thumping in her heart. He had a shock of black hair and large wide-set blue eyes. He was a big, well-built young man and handsome too.

Charlotte found herself looking into this face with disbelief. It couldn't be, but it was. She took a deep breath and composed herself outwardly, but inside she was in turmoil, and long-submerged memories welled to the surface.

"This is unreal," she thought. "This is the stuff of fiction. It can't be real. It can't be. But it is. It is real. So this is Angus. I know of you, Angus," she said to herself. 'The colour of your hair and eyes apart, you are so like him. You are the son he hadn't seen. You could be no one else. Oh God! How long is the arm of coincidence? Of all the young farmers in Scotland it had to be you and of all the ranches in Texas you had to come to this one."

"Rhona, will you show Angus around while I prepare tea - or perhaps you would like coffee? "

"Oh, tea will be very welcome, thank you."

"Yes I remember so fondly the afternoon tea in Scotland, with those delicious scones and jam and cream. They were lovely."

Charlotte made for the kitchen. She had to have time and space for a little while to sort things out for herself. She needed to be on her own to come to terms with the memories which were crowding in upon her.

"Why does this affect me so, and after all that time?" she said to herself. "I thought all of those memories were gone for ever. I thought all of those feelings I had for him had gone forever, but no! They are still there. Thank God I can occupy myself with present tasks. Maybe, with a little time, I can sort out my emotions. Perhaps it was just that first sight I had of Angus."

She recalled the figure of the big young man on the verandah. Just for one moment, as he stood there in silhouette, she was transported to a Scottish Highland glen where a lone Highlander stood on a rock by a pine tree and the sun behind him made a halo of his hair

Chapter Two

Through the trees the loch lay calm and indolent in the sunshine and the first tinges of purple heather could be seen on Ben Lomond. The day was balmy and Charlotte watched the spectacle and ceremony of her first ever Highland Games from her deck-chair in the shade of the oak tree. The little dancers enthralled and delighted her and the pageant and splendour of the pipe bands as they marched up and down in their richly coloured tartans would long be etched on her mind. Not even the babbling of Connie by her side could distract her. She watched as the little dancers with great skill and accuracy executed the intricate steps with incredible lightness of foot.

"Oh Charlotte," babbled Connie, "just look at that swell-looking guy, the one with the long hair and the beard. Isn't he just the handsomest man you ever did see? Oh, Ah do hope he wins, don't you?"

"I can't say I do, murmured Charlotte.

Charlotte's eyes were drawn to one athlete in particular. He was the youngest of them all and a picture of grace and strength. The sun tinted his dark auburn hair with gold as he sent the hammer soaring into the clear blue sky.

The young man won the event, but it was the one with the long hair who came swaggering over to them. He stood by them and smiled.

"Are you enjoying the games, ladies?"

"Gee, they are just swell," said Connie. "I just never did see such spectacle. I mean all those divine plaids. I'm sure they must have a special meaning somewhere."

"Oh, yes, they do. We refer to them as tartans. Each Scottish clan has it's own tartan, which is treasured and fiercely protected. Most clans have more than one tartan; they have a dress tartan, a hunting tartan, and many of them have an ancient tartan also. I'm wearing our hunting tartan today. Hunting tartans are usually predominantly green."

Charlotte formed the opinion that the little dancers must all be in dress tartan today, and full dress at that. The bobbing feathers on the bonnets and the lace jabots and cuffs and the brightly coloured hose had to be full dress. Nothing could top that.

"And those divine little dancers, Ah suppose they must have a history too."

"Oh they do. They do indeed."

He knelt down beside Connie, his hand resting lightly on her knee.

"All of the dances are rooted in history. We have a terrible and often violent history in the Scottish Highlands. The Highland Dances were at one time; performed only by men, but now the competitors are almost exclusively female and, for the most part, very young. The Highland fling, which was the first competition, was a dance of victory in battle. Traditionally, the ancient warriors and clansmen performed this dance on the small round shield called a targe which they carried into battle."

Charlotte could well understand the quick footwork and dexterity of the dancers when she learned that most targes carried a pinpoint sharp spike of steel projecting some five to six inches from its center. A false or careless step could be more than a little painful.

"The next one you saw was the Sword Dance or Ghillie Callum. This is an ancient dance of war of the Scottish Gael. It is said to date back to King Malcolm Canmore. A Celtic prince is said to have taken the sword of a chief he had subdued, crossed over it with his own on the ground before him, and danced over them both in exaltation. There is history behind every Highland dance."

"My! How interesting. You know you have made these games come alive for us. How can we ever thank you," gushed Connie, her eyes shining.

"My pleasure. I have to get back to work now. I hope we shall meet again later."

"Oh, Ah do hope so," Connie replied.

Connie saw little else of the games except the heavyweight events. She had eyes for nothing else. They were no less intriguing. The great handsome men in their swirling kilts threw the hammer, tossed the caber, putted the shot and threw great stones over a bar high above their heads. The sun was reflected from the sweat on their heavily muscled physiques as they pitted their strength as though in combat. Like the dances, many of the events had their origin in bloody and turbulent history.

"What the Hell am I doing here?" Charlotte asked herself again as she looked out of the window towards the loch. It was not that there was anything wrong with Loch Lomond or any other part of Scotland for that matter. The people were the kindliest and friendliest she had ever met and the scenery could not be bettered. She shook her head. She realised that her present mood was only part of the general malaise affecting her at present. She looked at the stack of expensive luggage and wondered why she had brought so much. She wondered why she had ever allowed Connie to persuade her to come on this trip in the first place.

"What you need is a break," Connie had told her after one of their heart-to-heart talks. "You need a break from Beaumont. You need a break from routine and above all you need a break from Tom and the boys. You need time and space to think what life is all about. You know, Charlotte, we all get a little dissatisfied with life now and again. What you want to do now is to stand back and have a look at your lifestyle. You are too close. You can't see the forest for the trees."

"Yes, I suppose so. I'll think about it."

"Think about it, my foot! You need a break and so do I. So let's just take ourselves off to Europe for a spell."

There were few problems. She and Tom did not talk too much these days anyway. He was too busy with his business interests.

"If you want this lifestyle you have to work your butt off to get it and even harder to maintain it," he said.

Their three teenage sons were at an expensive camp in Vermont for the summer. The endless round of bridge, tennis and cocktail parties and fund-raising events and the visits of the beautician and hairdresser, took up almost all of her time, but behind it all she felt a vague dissatisfaction. She felt there was something missing. There had to be something more to life.

Connie was the only person with whom she could discuss her innermost thoughts and even then only on a very selective basis.

"You should take a lover," Connie had advised her on one occasion, but the suggestion had little appeal for Charlotte. She was not all that keen on sex. At times she wondered how she ever came to have three teenage sons. She had got married when she was just turned nineteen and in the early days Tom had been an adventurous lover; but she had discouraged such practices. It was not in her

Bostonian upbringing to so indulge herself. Tom soon gave up and their love life became something quite mechanical. They were doing their marital duty towards each other and little else. No! The prospect of a lover did not rate highly ... and yet.

The picture of a big young Highlander kept intruding into her thoughts. She first saw him as they sat in the deck chairs under the oak tree. She could clearly recall the swirling kilt and the superb physique. Connie, in her usual gushing manner, insisted on his autograph when he won the event. Close up he was a spectacular young man. They had met again in the lounge bar after dinner. Connie had had her photo taken earlier in the day with the man she now called "her favorite athlete at the Highland Games".

"Just one for the album, you know," was her explanation.

The man had asked her to dinner, but she had declined. She did, however, agree to meet him for a drink after dinner. She insisted that Charlotte come too. Duncan - her friend - was bringing along a friend of his.

"No thanks, Connie. I don't need involvement of that kind."

"Oh, come on Charlotte - let your hair down just an mite or so. There's no need for you to get involved. Anyway, it's just that spectacular young man you admired so much this afternoon. His name is Hector."

She remembered the young man and agreed to come along. Duncan, Connie's friend, looked very well in his Highland dress and with his beard and long hair, but he was quite put in the shade by the young giant beside him. The young man was quiet and reserved and she noticed he drank only fruit juice. After a little, he lost his shyness and, despite his youth, chatted easily and was pleasant company.

Duncan leaned over and whispered in Connie's ear and then they both stood up.

"We're going for a stroll along the bonnie banks. Why don't you both come along too?" Connie suggested.

"No thanks. I'll finish my drink and then I think I shall go have a shower and write a few postcards," Charlotte replied.

She had no wish to cramp Connie's style in any way. They had made an agreement that anything, which happened during the trip, should be kept quite secret between them. The suggestion was Connie's and Charlotte concurred with it.

"It is nothing that will affect me anyway," she thought.

"And I shall keep Charlotte company while she finishes her drink, and then I too shall turn in," said Hector. It was quite some time before Charlotte and Hector made their way upstairs. Charlotte told him of her interest in the Scottish clans and tartans. Hector had lost his shyness and embarked on the history of his own clan. Like so many Highlanders he became eloquent when talking of his way of life.

"I come from Nether Lorne," he said. " The Macleans have always been associated with Argyll. The clan chief lives in Mull, in Duart Castle, but you find Macleans all over Argyll. Their origins are uncertain, like the origins of most clans. The one thing we can be almost certain of is that our origins are in Ireland, where most of the Scots originate. In their early days Macleans were priests and warriors. It was possible to be both in those days. Being priests, my ancestors were able to write and they managed to record quite a bit of their early history," he added. He had a deep soft pleasant voice and Charlotte listened in fascination as he told her of the turbulent history of his clan.

"Good Lord, would you look at the time!" he exclaimed as his eye caught the clock.

"You must be bored to tears listening to my ramblings," he said.

"Quite the contrary," said Charlotte. "It is a long time since I heard anything quite so interesting. I could listen to such tales for hours, but, yes, you are right. It is quite late, and I do have to write those post cards. "

"Well, I do have a book on the history of the Macleans. You are very welcome to borrow it."

"I'd love to, but I had better not. I would read all night and we do have quite an early start tomorrow, but thank you very much anyway. It is very kind of you."

"You are very welcome, and if you change your mind or if there is anything at all that I can do for you, I shall be only too pleased. So please do not hesitate."

"He is a courteous and, I think, compassionate young man," she decided.

Hector

This was the first of the Highland Games on the circuit for Hector. He missed the guidance of his trainer and mentor, Murdo, this year, but the other regulars on the circuit made him welcome. Hector sat now with Duncan MacIvor who was more renowned for his exploits off the field than his prowess on the field.

"I think I am going to have to look to my laurels." said Duncan.

"How's that?" said Hector

"You are attracting more than your fair share of the female interest."

"I hadn't noticed."

"Time you did. With your looks you can have your pick of what's going."

"You make us sound like a pop group with our groupies."

"Very similar, only on a lower key. We have our groupies too. They follow the circuit all summer. They are hooked on the romance of the big men in kilts. I play to the gallery all I can. You know, the beard and the longish hair and showing the hairy chest and flexing the muscles. You would be surprised how far that has got me. It is the cave man effect. It works almost every time."

"Is it working for you right now?" Hector asked with interest.

"Well, I'm hoping so. There was that American woman who asked to have her photo taken with me. There are definite possibilities there," said Duncan. "I'm meeting the girl and her friend for a drink tonight. Why don't you join us? I noticed the friend was taking maybe more than a casual interest in you."

"You are full of beans, Duncan."

"Not so. The practiced eye, you know. Come along anyway. What have you to lose? It could be quite fun. It could be something more than that."

"I think not, but I'll join you anyway. It's always nice to meet other people."

Chapter Three

The evening was warm and Charlotte had a shower and put on a short lightweight cotton nightdress with matching knee-length peignoir. She sat down by the open window. The mood for writing postcards had gone. The setting sun tinged the tops of the hills with pink. There was a magical stillness, which was broken only by the song of the birds as they settled down for the night.

A strange lassitude overcame her. Her thoughts wandered. It was a long time since she had allowed herself such a luxury. She closed her eyes and her thoughts roamed at will. She thought of the day she had just had and of the pleasant evening spent in the company of the big handsome young man with dark auburn hair.

"What a spectacular young man," she thought, "and so mature with it. He is just the kind of man a girl of any age could fall for very easily."

She sat up straight and shook herself.

"Ugh! Ugh! Charlotte," she said to herself. "Quite far enough. That sort of complication you do not need. He is just a boy. He is not much older than your own sons."

She thought instead of her life in oil-rich Beaumont. She found little comfort there either. There was little fulfillment in her life and the gnawing anxiety persisted. She wondered about her sons. Did they miss her? Did Tom miss her?

Probably not

"No one really needs me," she said to herself. "No one really needs me. Tom is all tied up with his oil deals. We seem to have grown more and more apart of late. The boys have their own lives too. They are going to need me less and less. My friends on the committees may gush about my success in fund-raising, but they know and I know that the fund-raising would go on even if I were never near it and are they really friends? I doubt it."

The idea unnerved her. There was a momentary panic. For the first time in many years she felt alone and vulnerable. The memories of the pleasant day were fast giving way to disturbing uncertainty. It was alien territory for Charlotte.

"What is all this about," she asked herself. "Why are you feeling like this?"

"I must think this through," she thought. "Yes, just what the hell are you doing here? I came to think things through. That's it. Things are not going well in Beaumont. Things are not going right in my marriage or with my family. I have just become conscious of that."

"No! That's not true either. I've been conscious of that for quite a time."

"What am I going to do about it?

"I don't know. I just don't know. I'll sleep on it. Maybe tomorrow … "

But the idea of sleep has gone.

"I must do something. Read a book. That's it, read a good book."

"You are very welcome to borrow it."

The words came back to her.

"No way, Charlotte," she reproached herself; still, she found herself crossing the hall.

He was almost asleep when the faint knock came to the door. He got up, wrapped a towel round his waist and opened the door. She stood there like an uncertain little girl.

"I can't seem to get off to sleep. I hope I'm not disturbing you. I, I thought I might after all borrow your book. I do hope I am not troubling you."

"No trouble at all, I assure you. Come on in. I'll get it for you. It's somewhere here in my bag."

He looked at her more closely as she entered the room. She looked so very different from the person with whom he had spent the evening. Gone was the self-assured and sophisticated woman he had left just a short time ago, and in her place was this apparently uncertain and vulnerable person.

"Are you all right?

"Yes. Yes, I'm all right."

Quite unaccountably, a tear rolled down her cheek.

He put his arm round her to comfort her and she buried her face in his chest. A fit of violent sobbing took hold of her and her body shook as years of tension and pent-up frustration and uncertainty and anxiety poured from her. He held her firmly and stroked her back in silence. Gradually the sobs subsided. She was conscious that she was holding on to his shoulders. She was conscious that he was holding her firmly and the soothing hands on her back drew all the pain and fear from her. Feeling disembodied, she half opened her eyes. She was unable to think. She felt the warmth of his closeness and she was conscious of a feeling of comfort. She raised her head and his lips brushed her forehead.

"I'm sorry. I don't know what came over me. I ... I ... "

"No need to be sorry. There is nothing like a good cry. A good cry can relieve all kinds of tensions. In your case it looks like that was long overdue."

He continued to hold her and to rub her back. The tensions had now largely left her. She was conscious of a sense of comfort and security in his arms. She burrowed her head deeper in his chest.

He lay on his back with his legs spread wide and his knees slightly raised and she was cradled between them. Her breasts rested on his chest and the hair tickled her nipples. He stroked her back and a great peace came over her.

"What happened? How did it come to happen?" she thought to herself.

"I don't quite know. I only know that I am immensely grateful that it did."

"You have no regrets?"

"God, no! Quite the opposite. Strangely, I don't. I should have, but no. The time will come, maybe quite soon, when I do; but for the moment, no."

He wiped a tear from the corner of her eye with the point of his little finger.

"Why the tear?"

"I don't know. Happiness. Gratitude also. It was a wonderful experience."

"I'm glad. It was a very wonderful experience for me too."

She lay across his chest and he held her tenderly in his arms.

"I should go now. My head is full of questions, but I should go."

"No! Please don't go. Stay. Stay with me tonight. Please. Please. It can be just as wonderful again. Please."

"I would not dare. There are all kinds of reasons why I can't."

She felt a bit lost and uncertain. Never before had she felt like that, but guilt was insinuating itself into her being.

"I am old enough to be your mother. I have a husband and three sons. I should never have come to your room. I'm sorry. I must go."

"No! Not like this. You can't go like this. You can't. Don't leave feeling bad. You mustn't feel bad about what has just happened. This need not mean that you do not love your husband and children. You most likely do love and miss them. I too have some one I love and miss. Everyone feels just a little lonely and vulnerable once in a while. Sometimes we need a comforting arm round us. It happens to everyone."

Now he was caressing her again and all of her senses swam and she clung to him. She knew then that she would stay.

The dawn of a new day was breaking and she felt a little afraid. The secure fences, which she had erected over the years, were tumbling about her. She snuggled closer to him and his arms held her more firmly. It had been a night of unbelievable tenderness.

"How had it happened? Was there regret?"

How had it come about she knew not, but there was no regret. She felt a strange sense of fulfillment. She felt a sense of freedom.

"I shall have to go soon, Hector. I know that my life will never be quite the same again. Tonight it is Edinburgh and back to the five-star hotel. Yesterday I almost insisted that we return to Glasgow when I saw this little hotel. Oh, I knew such places exist, but I never dreamed that I should stay in one. How glad I am now that we did. Do you always stay in hotels like this?"

"No, very seldom. I have an old van and a tent. The heavyweight athletes who follow the Highland Games circuit have to cover a lot of the country. This is how I earn my living just now. The Highland games are my main source of income, but I supplement it in other ways like fruit-picking and other things. I camp in beautiful little spots along the way and cook my food by the wayside and bathe in mountain streams and lonely lochs. It is a lovely way of life. You get time and space to think and there is such peace."

"It sounds wonderful and free and adventurous. So far removed from the life I've led. It is just that I have never known much else."

"Then come travel with me. Let's wander where our fancy takes us, just for a few days. After tomorrow, I have no more engagements for the next week. You have said that you have no fixed plans either. Try it, Charlotte. You have nothing to lose. I promise I shall protect you."

"And what of my friend? What shall I say to her?"

"Tell her you want a few days on your own to think. Let her take your car and baggage and you can meet up with her in Edinburgh next weekend. Leave all of your valuables with her and just take a few simple clothes and a pair of flat shoes. Let us be a pair of

Highland gypsies. We shall camp beside lonely lochs and we shall climb mountains and wander over hillsides."

"That sounds wonderful. I could never do that, but it sounds so beautiful. For the rest of my life I know I shall regret not having done this, but Hector, no! No, I can't."

"You must, Charlotte. You must. There will be no commitments. Just for a few days let us be together as fellow travelers. I sense you are at a crossroads and you feel a little lost and vulnerable. We all do now and again, Charlotte, especially when we are away from some one we love and miss. I too have a girl I love and miss. You can never know if what you are doing is quite right till you try something different - even for a little while. Let this be your something different."

They stopped on a quiet side-road. Nearby was a dark clump of trees and before them the stillness of a small loch. There was a perfect stillness. It seemed there was only them and God.

Connie had been incredulous.

"Charlotte you can't, not you. Are you feeling well?"

"I'm feeling fine. I just want to go off on my own. I just want time to think. After all, that is what you advised me to do. Look, why don't you just take the car and the baggage and go off to Edinburgh and check in at the hotel and I shall meet you there in five days? That is not long."

"Are you going on your own?"

"Of course. Who else is there? That's the whole idea."

"But where will you stay?"

"There are a few hotels. I don't know. I shall find one. I don't want much baggage. It ties one down so."

"Now I really think you are ill."

"Connie, honey, I assure you I am not in any way sick. It's just that I have had a chance to think, and, do you know, I enjoyed the experience? I'd just like to think some more."

Chapter Four

It had been difficult, but at last she persuaded Connie to set off by herself. Hector had to wait till the end of the games. He had many prizes to collect and it was after seven when he picked her up. The old white van had seen better days, but the seat was comfortable and she was off on an adventure, the likes of which she had never even dreamed.

"God! I feel like a pioneer setting out across the Mohave Desert for the Wild West," she thought.

Hector was singing an old Gaelic song. It was soft and pleasant. He looked across at her with affection in his eyes.

"What have we to worry about just now?" he asked.

"Quite a few things, I imagine."

"Name them."

"Well, there is … er … There is … " She hesitated.

"Ah! You have to think. Then it isn't worth the bother. Let's not bother worrying then. Sing me a wee song."

"I haven't sung in years. I think I have forgotten how."

"You never forget."

"I … I am afraid."

"For what? It isn't against the law, you know. Go on, just a wee song. Sing me one of those romantic Southern songs."

She began to sing 'Can't Help Lovin' That Man o' Mine' in a quavering voice, but gradually as the song progressed she let go and ended in gales of laughter. It was a long time since she had laughed like that too and they sang 'Loch Lomond' all the way along the loch and they talked and sang other Scottish ballads as they took the road northwards.

"And who is the girl you love and miss?" she asked him. "Or would you rather not talk of her? I shall understand."

"No, I don't mind talking of Bessie. She and I are neighbours or were neighbours. We have been in love for a long time now. We have a son called Angus. He is more than a year old, but I have never seen him. My parents are bringing him up."

"I don't understand, Hector. You hardly look old enough."

"Oh, I shall be nineteen by the end of this year. It is complicated, but I shall try to explain. It has all to do with our customs and the way we live in the Highlands."

"You see, Bessie and I grew up together. We have always been friends and we have always played together. The friendship grew into love and the play into something we had always been taught was wrong, but which neither of us could resist. It was as natural as the grouse on the moors and the deer in the glens. We were quite intemperate and very soon she was pregnant. She was more than four months pregnant when we discovered it."

"We were separated. She went to Edinburgh to have our child and I was sent to an aunt in Glasgow to finish my education. We have never seen each other since. Neither of us has been back to Nether Lorne. That is the way such matters are resolved in our communities."

"Our parents hope we'll forget each other in time, but they are wrong. We shan't. We are not supposed to communicate, but we do. We write to each other through a friend back home. It may take a little while but we shall be together one day soon. Of that we are sure."

"What a sad and touching story."

"Ah, yes. So it is, but it will have a happy ending. You'll see."

"Don't you feel guilty being with some one else?"

"Perhaps a wee bit. She will understand though."

"You will tell her?"

"Och, yes. I would never keep anything so important from her. She will know that I don't love her any the less for it. Just as you needn't feel you love your family any the less."

"That is very sweet and touching. How very mature you both are. I don' t think I shall ever get the courage to tell Tom anyway."

"You might. You never know."

He quickly set up the tent. It was quite big and roomy and he took out an airbed and blew it up. From the van he took out a stove and a bottle of gas and soon there was an aroma of sizzling steaks. She helped him put up the awning and set up the folding table and chairs. Soon a container of green salad appeared and then baked potatoes.

"Courtesy of the hotel," he commented. She had not been so hungry for a long time. Somehow, with the regime of the strict diet she had followed for so long she had got out of the habit. He made her promise to forget about "calories and such tripe" and enjoy her food.

He would not allow her to help with the cooking on this her first night.

The meal was like something she had forgotten from her childhood. It was accompanied by water from a spring, which was like nectar to her. The steaks were superb, and then came raspberries and cream. There was no coffee.

"You will have to get into the habit of tea except at breakfast."

It was past midnight when they got ready for bed and it was not yet dark. This far north, the nights never get completely dark in summer.

"I must get my sleeping pills from the van," said Charlotte.

"What do you want sleeping pills for?"

"I haven't been able to sleep without them for the last five years."

"Have you tried?"

"Well, no. I ..."

"What happens if you don't get to sleep? We shall lie in each other's arms and talk and what is wrong with that?"

"Not a lot that I can see, now that you mention it."

There was a time of exquisite tenderness and then he held her close and they lay like spoons. She was asleep immediately. It was light when she awoke. A shaft of early morning sun strayed into the tent through the open flaps. She stretched luxuriously.

"I could get used to this," she murmured.

He had coffee ready by the time she rose.

"Come, lazy bones!" he called to her. "Brush your teeth and come and have your furach."

"This is furach?" she said.

There was a big bowl of oatmeal and raspberries with cream.

"This is furach. It is just oatmeal, with honey soaked in milk overnight and eaten with soft fruit and cream next morning. I like raspberries best. Come and see what you think of it."

She scraped the bowl clean.

"That was utterly delicious. Is that how you always start the day?"

"Almost always."

"Little wonder you are so big and strong and handsome."

The golden mist over the loch was already clearing when they rose and it had lifted completely by the time they finished breakfast.

"Is the weather always like this?"

"No, I'm afraid it isn't very often as good as this. There is an area of high pressure over the country. We shall have gloriously warm weather for some time to come. It is ideal weather for hill climbing. Shall we start with this one here?"

"Hector, I can never climb a hill like that. I am an old lady, you know."

"An old lady you are not. After last night, that I know and know well."

The path up foothills was easy. He took her hand and then they came to the rough heather. It was steep here too. Charlotte stopped and looked up at the steep climb.

"Come. Sit on my shoulder. I shall carry you over the steepest part."

He easily hoisted her on to his shoulder.

"Oh, no, Hector!" she protested. "You can never carry me up there, big and strong as you are."

"Of course I can."

"No, Hector. No really, you must not."

"It is all right. As part of my training I carry a sack of oats up a hill. You are not so heavy as a sack of oats."

"Is that the only difference you have noticed?"

"No," he said, "I don't get all this backchat from the sack of oats."

She laughed and tweaked his cheeks. He loped easily over the roughest of the ground with the sure foot of a mountain goat.

At the top of the hill there was an old fort. The ramparts had all but disappeared in the mists of time and there was a smooth grassy hollow in the center. They sat and talked and drank water from a dewpond. It was ice-cold. When the day grew hot he spread his kilt on the short grass and they lay naked in the sun. He regarded her as she lay with her eyes closed. Yes! She was beautiful. She wore no makeup this morning. She had a very fine facial bone structure. She really needed very little makeup. Her breasts were firm for a woman of her age. She had taken care of her body. The waist was still slim.

She even slept for a little. When she opened her eyes he was standing on the rampart. She had seen little of the naked male body. She had never dreamed of seeing something so beautiful. Where the sunlight shone on the hair the curls were tipped with gold.

"He is like a god," she thought. "This is how the old Celtic gods must have looked."

The dark auburn hair gleamed in the sunlight and the muscular body was honed to perfection. As she gazed at him he turned to her. The large hazel eyes were soft and tender.

"You are a beautiful man."

"Thank you. I take that as a great compliment coming as it does from a beautiful woman, a very beautiful woman."

"I have never seen that combination of auburn hair and hazel eyes. Is it common among the Celts?"

"No actually - I think it is quite rare. The Macleans normally have black black hair and blue eyes. I am told that I am a throw-back to Appin Mary."

"And who was Appin Mary? She sounds romantic."

"Yes she was quite romantic."

"So how do you know that she was romantic?"

"Oh, such stories are passed down through the generations. I remember my father telling us about her when we were young sitting round the peat fire in the winter nights."

"Tell me of Appin Mary. I should love to hear the romance of the Highlands."

He sat with his back against a large standing stone and he drew her down on his knee. His arms were round her. The sun was warm on their bodies and a feeling of peace and languor overcame her. The soft deep voice caressed her senses.

"Appin Mary had been famous just over a century before. She had French blood in her. Her ancestors came over to Scotland with Bonnie Prince Charlie in 1745 at the time of the Jacobite rebellion. It isn't clear what part they took in the rebellion. They did settle in Appin and they seem to have been an industrious lot because they were prosperous, but there was some local difficulty there and they came and settled in Nether Lorne quite near the Maclean estate. They did not have too much luck in the early days. Her father died in a riding accident and her mother succumbed to tuberculosis within a year. Although she was still in her teens, Mary took up the reigns and looked after the estate and brought up her younger brothers and sisters. She could ride a horse better than any man and she could plough the straightest furrow in all Lorne. At lambing time she was to be seen out on the hills from daybreak - a big well-made girl of incredible beauty, striding over the hills high breasted and superb."

"She had a long mane of dark auburn hair and large hazel eyes. Almost all of the young men in the district tried to win her favours, but her indifference drove them to despair. When she was twenty, there was a late snowstorm, and while out on the hills rescuing the lambs she slipped on the frozen snow and fell to the bottom of a glen. She was discovered there unconscious, by one of her neighbours.

"Angus Maclean was a gentle giant of a young man. At first he thought she was dead and then he felt the faint heart beat. He carried her to the nearby bothy and laid her by the peat fire. The embers were barely smoldering. He threw a heap of peat into the fire and blew violently into it to coax the feeble flame and then he turned his attention to the unconscious form. She was blue with cold. He tore the sodden clothes from her, laid her on the bed and covered her over with blankets. He rubbed her vigorously with a rough towel, but there was no response. The fire was still barely smoldering. She needed warmth and quickly. He took off his clothes, pulled the blankets over them and he covered her with the warmth of his nakedness. He placed the frozen fingers in his armpits. He held the ice cold feet between his feet and he rubbed her back.

"After what seemed an age the chill left her body and a faint moan escaped her lips. She opened her large eyes. For a moment she was startled and then she remembered the fall.

'Where am I? Angus Maclean?' she asked.

'Yes. You are in the bothy. I found you unconscious.'

"He was a young man of little experience where women were concerned. His face reddened as the reality of the situation struck him.

'I ... Er, I ...' He stammered. 'You needed warming urgently. The fire was almost out. There was no other way. I ... I am sorry. I shall ... '

He made to move, but she held him close.

Thank you. Thank you very much. I know that you have saved my life, but please I am still cold.

He continued to hold her close to him and to rub her back and then he felt her arms go round his neck, and time and the world ceased to be.

"They were my great-great-grandparents. They were married that summer. Their progeny were numerous, but, until I came along, none had inherited her looks."

"Oh, what a lovely story. It must make you feel a part of history. We lack history of this kind in the States."

"Yes, but I fear it might be short-lived history. I am about to die of hunger. Are you hungry?"

"Hector, I am ravenous," she said.

"Then let's go back to the camp and eat."

Chapter Five

"Now, where is my mirror? I must look a mess. I just realised I don't have on my makeup and I only drew a comb through my hair this morning and, oh my God, look at my nails!"

Hector put his arms round her waist and held her close.

"You look beautiful, so no make up. If you must, a little lipstick and a little cream to prevent sunburn, but no make up and no mirrors and life will be so much easier if you cut your nails." He brought her a pair of nail scissors.

"You do it, Hector. I know it is necessary, but I spent years growing those nails. I don't have the heart."

"It will be better. You will see." He cut them medium long.

He took a fishing rod from the back of the van and they went fishing in the loch. He taught her how to cast and soon she had the thrill of catching her first trout. She was like a child in wonderland. She caught two more. They were nice fat brown trout and very soon he had them gutted and cleaned and, now coated with oatmeal, they were sizzling in a frying pan. On the other burner was a pot of new potatoes boiling steadily.

"Oh, I had forgotten just how good food could taste. This is superb and this is a heavenly place. Oh, Hector, let's stay here for ever!"

"You won't be much of gypsy sitting in one place for ever. There is so much more of Scotland that I want to show you. You will enjoy it just as much I assure you."

"I shall be sorry to leave this spot. I caught my first trout here among other things."

"There are better trout in the West."

"Isn't that too near to your home?"

"No. We shall head further north. We'll go by Appin and perhaps Ardnamurchan. Come, let's pack up and head west. That is the land of magic."

They meandered through mountain, hillside and glen and they strolled hand in hand along silver beaches. The sun shone and the days were balmy. They loved and they talked freely and they explored bodies and minds. They kept to the byways and for much of the time they had the world to themselves.

She turned her face towards him. The bracken fringe around the corrie was darkly etched against the blue sky. She was slowly descending from a pinnacle of ecstasy. The sensations were still with her. They were etched in her mind as clearly as the bracken against the blue sky. He had brought her to this pinnacle very slowly. She could still feel the sensual probing tongue and the endless caressing.

"Oh, Hector," she whispered.

He drew his bottom lip along her jawbone.

"Happy?"

"Supremely. I never imagined it could be like this. There seems to be no limit to the frequency and the intensity. How do you come by this capacity for making love and with such expertise?"

"That is a difficult one to answer. I don't completely understand how it comes about, Charlotte. Everything was fairly normal till almost three years ago when I had just turned fifteen. Something went completely awry with my body chemistry. It almost drove me mad till I had my first sex experience with Bessie. Oh God! When I think back on those first months, Charlotte. I was insatiable and Bessie little better."

"Was that when you gained your expertise?"

"No, that was much more youthful energy and ardor and just sheer joy of living. There was not a lot of expertise involved. That came later with Sadie."

"And who is Sadie? You have all kinds of mysterious women in your life."

"There is nothing mysterious about Sadie. She is the wife of my cousin Donald. I lived with them for six months when I was sent to Glasgow."

"And you seduced her."

"No! In fact, she seduced me, and I shall be forever grateful to her. She was my savior in many ways. She spared me a great deal of heart-searching and hang-ups."

"And?"

"And what?"

"And so tell me about Sadie."

"Hmm. Why not? It might spare you a few hang-ups too."

"I find it hard to describe Sadie. She is a highly intelligent, yet practical woman and she had a down-to-earth philosophy and openness, which was very attractive. I think it was her philosophical outlook on life, which I found most intriguing. She spoke quite frankly of how near she came to nymphomania. To her, it was something she had to live with, and, as was her wont, live with it she did, just as well as she possibly could. Sadie was one of those people of whom society disapproves, and yet she was someone special. She enriched the lives of everyone who was near her. She certainly enriched mine. She also recognised that I came somewhere near to a condition of Satyriasis."

"What's that?"

"The equivalent, in men, of nymphomania in women. I cannot make up my mind if it is a case of it takes one to know one, but Sadie somehow recognised the fact that I had a higher than normal need of sex and she told me that since I do, I might as well do it properly. She taught me a lot. In many areas of my young life I have been fortunate enough to meet people who have helped me greatly. There is Murdo MacLeod who gave me such wonderful coaching in Highland heavyweight athletics and there is also Sadie. She taught me about sex as no other person I could imagine, and she taught me how to face up to problems in life. She made me aware of the needs of my partner as well as my own and above all that I must never feel guilty."

"Do you ever feel guilty?"

"No. I don't think so. Traditionally the Presbyterian religion frowns on sex outside of marriage, but I can't believe that God would have given mankind anything so wonderful as sexual intercourse if he did not mean people to practice it widely. Socially there are obligations, but within that framework I wouldn't have any guilt complexes."

" That is a very mature point of view. You are a very mature person. How does that come about?"

"I don't really know. My brothers tease me about my outlook on life. They call me old sober sides. It may be because I became a father at such a young age, or maybe it is just the way I am made. I just don't know. Perhaps it explains my attitude to sex."

"So what do you do when you can't get sex?"

"I do without. Don't worry. We shall have sex at your pace. I want you to enjoy yourself."

She hugged him.

"Sex the way you perform is something I am coming to enjoy very much."

30

"What now, Charlotte?" she asked herself. "Where do you go from here?"

She sat with her back against a pine stump and watched the seals on the rocks a little way offshore. They were basking in the warmth of the afternoon. Nearby two otters were playing in the sun. They slid down a smooth rock into the water and then climbed back up the rock again. They played and played.

Hector had gone on foot to the village for bread. She thought of him fondly.

"He is truly a remarkable young man," she thought. "It isn't just his looks, although he is certainly the best-looking man I have ever met, or his skills as a lover, it is his maturity and his wisdom too. I am almost twice his age and yet I am learning so much about life from him. Not only that, he is so sensitive. I know that going for bread is not that urgent right now, but he knows that I needed time on my own, and I do. I need that very much just at this moment."

She thought of the conversation they had just had. She had been explaining how she spent her days and she described her social life and the fund raising-activities in which she took part.

"Very admirable," he remarked. "And what do you do with the money you raise?"

"Oh, we give it to various charities."

"Do you ever meet the people who receive the money you raise?"

"Well, no, not really. You see, we just raise the money."

"Don't you think it would be nice to meet some of them at least? They might welcome the chance to say thank you."

"Yes, I can see that now. Our charity does seem a bit cold."

To change the subject, she talked of her sons. He wondered about the wisdom of the level of provision and protection that they offered their children.

"Don't you think that in some ways you are depriving them?"

"That is a ridiculous suggestion."

"It is not. They have to make their own way in life. Even if it were not for Bessie and Angus, I would still have been here. I could just as well stay at home and work on the farm, but I choose to travel and I regard it as a challenge and as training for the future. You might be depriving them of that opportunity."

"You could be right. It would certainly lighten the load on Tom's back."

She was faced now with the stark reality of the shallowness of her lifestyle. There was no defense that she could offer. Without the protection of the beautician and the hair stylist and deprived of make up, she was forced to look at her lifestyle and herself in the cold light of day.

"Yes! Where are you going, Charlotte? God, I don't know. Does anyone need me any more? Maybe not! No one is indispensable. Does anyone want me any more? Not as I was. Who would want a hard-bitten, brittle, shallow woman? Oh God I didn't intend it that way. I was only trying to do my best for everyone. It is just that I didn't know any other way."

She looked down the road and she saw his kilted figure in the distance. In her bare feet she ran to meet him and threw herself, sobbing, into his arms. He held her close and kissed her hair and rubbed her back. After some time her sobs subsided.

"I have some lovely fresh bread," he said. "Come, we'll go back to camp and make some tea. We'll talk some more later."

"I have never done this before," she said.

"What's that?

"Been intimate with a man like I am being with you."

He had, from the start, encouraged her to caress and fondle him.

"Mind you, apart from Tom there has never been any other man in my life."

"Do you enjoy being this intimate?"

"Hmm ... yes."

"Then you should do it more often. I am sure it will be well received."

"Shall I ever get the chance?" she wondered to herself.

This was their last night. Till then she had not discussed her marriage so openly. Now, she told him of Tom's early adventurous overtures and of her reserve and how their sex life had become just a routine, like so much of their lives.

"Does he like his work?"

"I suppose. No, I don't think he does. I think that deep down all he ever wanted to do was to ranch. Oh dear, oh dear! I think I have been a great fool."

He took her in his arms.

"No! You have been misguided, mistaken too, perhaps. It isn't a crime to make a mistake, even a big one, but there isn't much merit in continuing with a mistake. Sometimes a change is necessary."

"That is putting it mildly. I begin to see things from Tom's point of view. Little wonder he lost interest when I spent about an hour every might taking off make up and putting on night creams, hormone creams and you name it. It is kind of surprising we ever got round to sex at all."

"It isn't too late."

"I wonder?"

"It isn't."

"What would you do in my shoes?"

"I would call him and ask him to join you right away."

"That is not possible. He is working on a big oil deal. He is working on taking over a rival. It will keep Tom full out for years to handle it."

"It will take him even further from his ranch."

"He isn't big enough on his own. You have to be big to survive in that world today."

"Does he want to? There are other worlds."

"Yes, there are. I discovered another world - why couldn't he? He'd have to sell out."

"Would he make a lot of money?"

"A few million, I guess."

"How much would a ranch cost?"

"A good one would cost about a million, I would guess."

"You are a smart girl, Charlotte Benson. I bet you could come up with a lifestyle that would suit you all and something that you could manage very well on the odd million or two that you would have left over; and, by the way, a ranch is great place to bring up young men."

"You are not joking."

"I am not joking. Think about it."

"How come you are so wise? You are wise far beyond your years. You are far more wise than I am."

"I suppose! I think it is because I am on my own a lot. You get time to think, and I have never been one to just accept things because they are fashionable or because other people think or act in a certain way. It is not always a comfortable existence, but it is always interesting. Often it is exciting."

"I seldom get the chance or even take the chance to think. I have thought more about life in the last few days than I have done in the last few years."

"Did you enjoy the experience?"

"Yes, I did.

"Think how it would be in the early morning or late evening on horseback, on your own ranch and all by yourself. With the solitude and stillness the rest will come as sure as the sun will rise. Even if you don't always want that, then it will be just as good riding out with Tom."

"God, yes! Tom. When I think how I have treated that guy. You know, Hector, despite our fling I do love the man."

"I'm sure you do."

"Yes, I want to make it up to him. When we get together it is going to be like meeting a stranger?"

"He'll be the same. It is you who is going to be the stranger."

"How right you are. It will be like on a honeymoon. How do I tackle that?"

"You trust to your instincts. It is all there, Charlotte, and what is there is good."

The rising sun tinged the banks of mist with gold and he loved her long and tenderly and then she rose and washed and dressed. They had furach and coffee.

They were camped on a hillside in a picturesque little glen. Just down below them in the village a train was waiting, it seemed impatiently, at the station.

"Let's part just here. I shall manage to find my way to the station. It is only a little way. I want to leave you where I will want to remember you - in the wild country."

"Are you sure?"

"Yes."

"All the best."

"And to you."

They kissed only briefly.

Before she boarded the train she looked up to the hillside. There was a golden eagle soaring in the blue sky, its wings tipped with light. He stood on a rock beside a pine tree - a lone Highlander. The sun behind him made a halo on his hair.

"That is how it should be," she thought.

Chapter Six

There was a breeze, which kept the open verandah cool, and Charlotte had set tea out there. Through the arches the rolling landscape spread out before them. Angus came out and wandered over to the edge of the verandah. He had changed into a pair of jeans and a light shirt. He nodded his head sideways.

"They told me it was big. I just hadn't realized how big."

He sat down at the table in an easy manner.

"You know, I have been so longing to see this. When our Young Farmers Club got the invitation from the Texas 4H for an exchange visit, I thought about it for a few days. It was my father who made me aware of just what a chance it was. I am so glad now that I took the chance. It is very kind of you to have us."

"Not at all. We are very happy to have you here."

They rose from the table and Rhona looked Angus over from head to toe.

"Hmm. Not bad. Perhaps an added touch here and there."

She took a red spotted bandanna and knotted it around his neck, and, from the stand, she took a battered old Stetson and placed it on his head. These added touches instantly transformed him into a rancher.

"Magic," said Rhona. She was thrilled with the transformation. "You are just about ready to take on the longhorns."

"Now, Rhona, remember that Angus has had a long flight."

"Oh, he'll be all right. I'm taking him out over the range. Maybe we shall get as far as Willow Creek. That's where my brother Mike ranches," she explained to Angus. " It touches on to this ranch."

"Don't let her tire you out Angus," Charlotte warned.

"I'll be all right. I'm really keen to get going. I want to learn as much as I can about life on a ranch. I would like to be able to handle a horse properly and rope a steer and many other things. I hope you will teach me, Rhona."

Charlotte saw her daughter glow with pride. This big man was asking her to teach him how to handle a horse and how to rope a steer. It was obviously a matter of immense gratification to her.

"I'll teach you all I can, Angus, and with the greatest of pleasure."

She took his arm and led him to the barn. Charlotte waved them off as they trotted down the road.

"Shall we see some longhorns?" asked Angus.

"Not tonight. They are out in the far range. They are hardier than the rest and withstand the heat better. That is why we put them out in the drier ranges. We shall see them tomorrow. Tonight we shall have a look at the Santa Gertrudis cattle."

"Oh, great. I read a little about them. They sound a bit exotic. How did they get that name?"

"Like so many other things, it is tied up with the King Ranch. Almost all of the ranching history in Texas is in some way tied up with the King Ranch."

"The Santa Gertrudis was developed by crossing Indian Brahman cattle with British Shorthorns. In 1920, years of experimentation culminated with the birth of Monkey, a deep red bull calf. Monkey became the foundation sire for not just a superior line of cattle, but an entirely new breed. In 1940, Santa Gertrudis was recognized by the U.S. Department of Agriculture as the first beef breed developed in the United States. "

"Well done, the King Ranch."

"Yes, and there is a second breed being developed on the ranch, the King Ranch Santa Cruz. This breed represents more than seven years of intense research and development aimed at creating a more market-acceptable beef animal that produces superior results as both a feeder and seed stock animal. Along with King Ranch professionals, twenty-six professors from fourteen universities participated in the formulation of the master-breeding plan, which produced the King Ranch Santa Cruz. The new cattle is a composite breed: half Santa Gertrudis, quarter Red Angus, and quarter Gelbvieh. We don't have any Santa Cruz, but we are quite heavily into the Santa Gertrudis. Both those breeds were developed for the hot, dry and often humid climates of West Texas."

"He seems to have been quite a man, Mr. King."

"Captain King to you, Sir; and, yes, he was quite a man. The King Ranch was founded in 1853 after Captain Richard King traveled north from Brownsville to attend the Lone Star Fair in Corpus Christi. King's route took him through the Wild Horse Desert where he encountered the Santa Gertrudis Creek, the first live water he had seen in a hundred and twenty-four miles. The creek was an oasis shaded by large mesquite trees and offered protection from the sun as well as cool, sweet water to refresh the traveler.

"At the Fair, King met a friend of his, Texas Ranger Captain, Gideon K. 'Legs' Lewis, and he described his journey north. He was very interested and they formed a partnership to establish and operate a livestock operation with its headquarters on this Creek. The land the partnership purchased was the fifteen thousand, five hundred acre Spanish land grant known as the Rincon de Santa Gertrudis.

"King's first effort to set up a cow camp and tame the Wild Horse Desert was the beginning of a dream he would pursue the rest of his life. In the years since King's death, King Ranch has been a bellwether of America's ranching industry - the founder of two major American beef breeds, a producer of some of the all-time top running and performance horses, and a source of technology that has led to many significant advances in livestock and wildlife production and management. Because of this vision, King Ranch is generally recognized today as the birthplace of the American ranching industry. King Ranch continues to play a significant role as a leader in the multinational agricultural business world and energy development."

"Wild Horse Desert and the Rincon de Santa Gertrudis, that is stuff of pure romance. Don't tell me you don't have romance and history in Texas."

Charlotte was there to greet them when they returned.

"How did you enjoy the ride, Angus?" she called.

He walked rather stiffly on to the verandah.

"Oh, oh," was his response as he placed his hands on his buttocks. "I kind of think I am a bit saddle-sore, Ma'am."

"Ah, poor Angus - you've been over- doing it. That is so easy to do. I think this calls for a good hot tub and some rubbing alcohol and you should be all right by morning. Really, Rhona, you mustn't overwork our guest."

"Oh, he'll survive. He's a big boy and anyway it is just as much his doing as mine. I did suggest we turn back, but he just had to see the Santa Gertrudis. I think he's in danger of becoming as obsessed with ranching as I am."

"Oh dear," mused Charlotte. "Anyway, I think a drink will help too. Scotch or Bourbon, Angus?"

"I think I'll try the Bourbon, thanks."

Charlotte appeared with a tray.

"There are two lots of alcohol here, Angus," she began. "The one in the glass is for the inside. You drink that one while you lie in your hot tub. The one in the bottle is for the outside. After you dry off, you apply that liberally to where you hurt most. It may sting a little, but don't worry, it will do you no end of good. Now off you go and have a good soak. Dinner will be ready in about an hour."

"Thanks," he said. "You are very kind. I somehow think insomnia will not be one of my major problems tonight."

He took the tray and made for the bathroom with a shambling wide-legged gait.

A crease appeared on Charlotte's forehead. There was something troubling her. It was not just the ghost from the past, which had almost caused her to faint. A thought, an idea was hovering just on the edge of her consciousness. It remained elusive. She could not quite bring it into focus.

"I shall ride out to the lone pine tomorrow" she thought. "Maybe the answer will come to me there."

They were out early next morning. Charlotte could hear them fix breakfast before she got up. There was a lot of earnest discussion, but there was a lot of laughter too.

"And why not?" thought Charlotte. "They have a lot in common. Despite their tender years, they are both running their own operations. They are both young and fit and very active and they are both highly intelligent individuals. It should be an interesting week," she decided.

They were down by the barn when she brought her coffee out to the verandah. The sun was just up and the morning was fresh and bright, with dew still on the grass. She loved this time of day, when the world was young and fresh and the clean clear smells of morning had still to evaporate in the heat of day.

Angus was having his first lessons with the lasso. Rhona sent the noose of the rope snaking out and expertly lassoed the fence-post.

"This rope seems to have a will of its own," said Angus. "I just can't seem to get it to go where I want it to go."

"It is called a lariat and keep trying. It will all come together."

It took Angus six tries before he succeeded. He earned a solid pat on his back. They led the horses out from the barn. Rhona easily swung herself into the saddle while Angus watched in awe and admiration. She had to repeat the action twice while he tried to copy her, and then they were off down the road, riding close together.

For Angus the trip was more than just a holiday. He was an earnest young man. He was keen to learn all he could about Texas in general and ranching in particular. He wanted to know how things were done and he wanted to be able to do them and, as was his way, he wanted to do them well. Rhona took her task as his guide and mentor to heart. She felt very proud to be his mentor. She thought back and remembered how her father had set about teaching her. She decided to do something similar with Angus.

"I guess I shall have to speed up the process a little," she decided.

He was tall, dark, and very attractive, and, subconsciously, that added spice to her efforts. She took a delight in teaching him how to handle a workhorse.

The swirling dust was everywhere and he coughed and spluttered and wiped the sweat with the back of his hand. The smell of sweaty cattle and singed hair assailed his nostrils. He could feel the palpable fear of the steer as he held it down while she branded it. She did this with the same calm efficiency she applied to everything she did.

"All right, cowboy, I think we can have a break. The horses need a break anyway." He was full of admiration for her.

"Well, bully for the horses. They are not the only ones needing a break."

Angus patted his horse's neck and ran his hand over its sweat-stained flank. He wiped the sweat from his face with his bandanna.

"You know, I always thought those things were for decoration."

"Not much chance of that, except in Western films. Life on a ranch is pretty basic. There is not too much place for adornment."

They tied the horses loosely and left them to graze and then sat down on a blanket under a tree. She took a thermos of coffee and a bundle of thick sandwiches from her saddlebag.

"What, no chuck-wagon?" he asked.

"No chuck-wagons, cowboy. They too belong in history now, though they were once the most important item of equipment at roundup or on cattle drives, but that is all now part of our history."

"Is that an area of interest for you?"

"Yes, as a matter of fact it is."

"Then tell me about the chuck-wagons. I did manage to read up a bit before I came out. Not that there was very much available. Just enough to really whet my appetite, but I loved what I did manage to read about Texas."

"We don't have the long history that Scotland does. Mom goes quite lyrical when she talks of that."

"Maybe it is not as long-lived as ours, but it none the less interesting and dramatic too."

"Well, to tell you about the chuck-wagons. It is possible that more is written about the chuck-wagon than any other aspect of the early cattle ranching scene."

"The chuck-wagon was a mess-wagon that carried the cooking outfit, food, and supplies when cowboys drove the herds up the cattle trails of the West or gathered their own cattle during the fall and spring roundups on the home ranch. The wagon was the cowboy's 'home on the range' and, more often than not, the centerpiece of the drive or roundup. The chuckwagon is credited to Texas cattle-baron Charles Goodnight. In Eighteen sixty-six, Goodnight reworked an old Army wagon, selected primarily because it had extra heavy-duty iron axles. The design became so popular that cattle outfits all over the West began to copy it, each ranch making only slight changes. Eventually, the idea became a commercial success and chuck wagons were produced by several wagon-builders, including the Studebaker Company, which sold the wagons for seventy-five dollars to a hundred dollars"

"On the trail, the chuck-wagon followed behind the remuda as it trailed the main herd. It was the moving 'throne' for the cook. It boiled down to the fact that the best cooks attracted the best men on a cattle drive. The competition was fierce."

"What is a remuda?"

"Oh, that is just an extra herd of saddle horses, "

"Today, the big cattle drives are over, and the cook spends most of the time at the ranch headquarters kitchen, where the facilities are convenient and modern. But the cook still rules the realm and still wants to be treated with respect. The meals are more varied, better balanced, and far more nutritious. Hungry cowboys have to be fed. There is no substitution for the good solid food. Ranch work remains hard, the weather is still unpredictable, and the hours haven't changed a lot. Good food is a must in those circumstances. And that, dear Angus, is the story of the chuck-wagon."

"Smashing stuff. I haven't noticed a bunk-house on your ranch."

"No! Our cowboys have their families with them. They get back home every night and so we don't need a bunkhouse. Juan, the foreman, can put up a single cowboy or two if necessary. Just occasionally we do hire an extra hand. The other hands all have their families right here on the ranch. My father invested in good housing just after he bought the ranch. It was a wise investment, because all of our hands have been with us for years. With paddocks, the need for large numbers of hands has disappeared. We still have quite a large piece of open range but that is becoming less common now. Added to that we have cattle shutes and we tend to use them for steers over five hundred pounds, but the old-fashioned way of rounding up calves, roping and branding them takes a lot of beating."

"Your history means quite a lot to you, doesn't it?"

"Yes," she replied with a kind of dreamlike expression, "it does. My father instilled a love of the history of these parts. It was something of a passion for him and quite a bit seems to have rubbed off on me. It wasn't the only thing he taught me. He taught me a great deal besides. Just about everything I know, when I come to think of it."

"He too means a lot to you, I think."

"Does it show that much? I love my mom dearly, very dearly, but I adored my father. I just adored him. I always did. There is no other way I could say it. It wasn't just that he was my father. He was the kind of man I would have adored anyway. I guess I am just specially fortunate that he was my father too."

"And that's the way it should be."

"So where are the other hands today?"

"They are all way over the other side of the ranch doing almost exactly what we are doing here. This is a small bunch here. I chose them because it gives me a chance to give you a bit of practice."

"Thanks a lot. I greatly appreciate what you are doing for me, and, quite incidentally, I greatly admire your skills. In fact, I think you are just hell on wheels."

"Thanks, cowboy. That means a lot to me."

Chapter Seven

She sat for longer than usual over her coffee. She was in a contemplative mood. The arrival of Angus had unleashed a whole host of memories, which Charlotte could not exclude from her mind. They kept crowding in upon her, and then there was this elusive thought somewhere on the edges of her consciousness. She thought fondly of Tom.

"Oh, Tom," she said. "How glad I am that we took that trip. What memories I have of those four weeks. That was when we fell in love all over again."

The train took two hours to reach Edinburgh. She spoke to no one. It was a time for reflection. By the time the train arrived there, in mid morning, Charlotte was clear in her mind what she wanted from life. It was something vastly different from her views of even a week ago.

The reservations had been made and her baggage was already in her room. She decided to freshen up before meeting Connie. She looked at the pile of baggage. Somewhere there was a case of cosmetics and beauty aids. She poured water into the basin, splashed her face, put on a little lipstick and ran a comb through her hair. She picked up the telephone and called Connie's room.

"I'll be there right away, Darling."

There was a knock on the door and she rose to open it with not a little trepidation.

"Oh, Darling, I have been just so worried."

"Then I am sorry you took the trouble, Connie. There was nothing whatsoever to worry about. I have been very well."

"You do look very healthy, I must admit; but if I may say so, perhaps a little under-groomed. Not to worry, Darling, we shall just ring down for an appointment. Do you know, they have the most divine beauticians right here in the hotel."

"Then you can save your breath and my money, Connie. This is the way I am and this is the way I intend to stay. I am perfectly happy with my appearance."

"Well, I do understand if you have gone through a kind of spiritual thing, Darling. I mean, we all do from time to time, but you will be over it in a day or two, so not to worry."

"I shan't. I shan't either worry or be over it."

"Oh well," said Connie with resignation, "it will be all right on holiday, I suppose."

"It will be all right after that too."

"But not when you go back to Beaumont. I mean, our circle. They just won't like that sort of thing."

"Well, if I may quote Ret Butler: 'Frankly, my Dear, I don't give a fuck.'"

"Charlotte! How could you? I just know now you are ill. I blame myself for letting you go out on your own."

"Connie, sweetheart, I have never in my life felt better either in mind or in body. For the first time I feel as though I am some one on my own account. I appreciate your concern. Believe me I do, but I have just remembered something. I have just remembered the time difference. I need to call Tom. There is something, which I want to say to him and it just can't wait. He may even be in bed already, but I have to try to get him. You wouldn't mind giving me a few minutes of privacy. I promise I shall come and fetch you the minute I am through."

Connie sat in her room and wondered what had happened to her friend. She had to admit she looked the picture of health - even without makeup - and that was something she had never seen in all the time she had known her. It wasn't just that, though. The eyes sparkled and she positively glowed. It was something kind of spiritual. Well, she would find out in time.

"You are through to Beaumont now," said the receptionist. Tom's voice came on the line.

"Charlotte, is something wrong? Why are you calling me at this time of night? Are you all right?"

"Tom! How nice to hear your voice. Yes, I am fine. I just kind of missed you. I wanted to talk to you and find out how you are faring, and how the business deal is going?"

"Charlotte, are you sure you are all right?"

She sounded different. Never in her life had she expressed any interest in his business. Never had she called him to ask how he was.

"Yes, I am fine. Please don't worry about me. It's just that I've had time to think some things out. There are things I want to talk to you about and I want to see you too. How is the deal going?"

"We are stuck right now."

"What's wrong?"

"What's wrong is that he wants to take me over and I want to take him over and it is all-out war."

"Let him have it."

"I don't get you."

"Oh, Tom, I don't know how to say this. It's just that I feel we have been drifting apart and that is the last thing I want to happen. Tom, I love you. Maybe I haven't taken time to tell you that of late, but I do. I truly do and that's why I say let him have it. Give him the lot, but screw him for every cent you can. Listen honey! I love you. I want you. If you get control, you get the coronary and the ulcers. I don't want that. I want you and I want you healthy and relaxed and fit and I love you. Let him have it and come over here and join me. Maybe I am not making too much sense just now, but I know that what I am saying is right. Trust me, Tom. What more can I say?"

"What you are saying sounds just fine, but what of the kids and what will we do?"

"Whatever you like. As for the kids, let them find their own feet. We can't hang on to them forever. We have to let go. It isn't fair to them."

"I just ..."

He hesitated. She sounded so different. What had happened to her in those few days she had been away? He could almost swear he had heard her use the word 'screw'. As she was talking to him, the realisation came to him that he rather liked what he was hearing. Somehow, deep down, he felt he should trust her.

"This is all very sudden, Charlotte. I think I like what you say, though. I just find it a bit unexpected. I have difficulty in believing what I am hearing."

"You'd better believe it, Honey."

"You want me to let that son of a bitch have the lot?"

"Yes! The coronary. The ulcers. The lot. Honey, trust me - it will work out for the best. I promise. We have a lot to talk over, maybe a whole lifetime. It will take a little while."

"And you want me to come over there?"

"Yes, I do. I love you and I want you."

"Honey, you got a deal. I think I love you a lot too, Babe. Just stay there in the hotel. I'll be in touch later. I'll see you in a day or two."

He hung up.

Yes, he had predicted this. It would work out just as he had said. She wanted to tell him so. She wanted this very much, but she knew they would never meet again.

"Maybe just as well. I am screwed up enough. God, life can be a bitch," she thought. "Well, maybe not. Now what was it he had said?"

"It would be foolish not to change, now you have thought of something better. Before, you were just misguided."

God, and how misguided! But he was right. She must not miss this chance.

"Thank you, God. I'll try. Meantime there's Connie. Even Connie can't faze me now."

She was calm with an inner certainty that she was doing right. It was a feeling she had never had before.

"Thank you. Wherever you are, thank you," she whispered. "I have to put you to the back of my mind. I can never put you out of it. I have no regrets. I am ever grateful, but I cannot again consciously think of you. I know you will understand."

She sighed deeply and went to find her friend.

"I'm sorry, Connie. I should never have used that word. You don't deserve it."

"Oh, that doesn't matter, not at all. I've heard the word before. It was just a little surprising coming from you. That's all."

"Then I'm glad. Now tell me what you have been doing in the last few days."

"Oh, Charlotte, I ran into an old friend I used to know in the little town where I was born. She lives in Dallas and what she has to say about that social scene makes our little Beaumont sound like Hicksville. And I mean it. Just wait till you meet her. She will just sweep you off your feet. In fact, she is going to Paris in two days and has asked us along too. Isn't that the most exciting thing? And we've been buying up the most heavenly plaids and cashmeres here and you have a lot of buying to do to catch up and Paris is only two days away. I'm just so looking forward to it."

"I'm glad for you that you have been having a nice time, Connie, but I can't go with you to Paris. You just go ahead, though. I have to stay here to meet Tom. He is coming in two days."

"You mean here, Tom is coming here?"

"Yes. I called him and asked him to join me here. I just want to see him again. He said yes."

"Gee, Honey, you sure have changed. I don't know what happened, but it has turned you right upside-down. You won't mind if I go off to Paris?"

"No, not at all - and enjoy yourself."

"By the way, I thought Tom and my Bob were locked in some big deal and it was war to the death."

"Yes, I believe so, but it looks like one of them has lost. I didn't ask."

"Very wise, Darling. It is all so boring. One ends up with the oil and one with the money. It doesn't seem to matter much, which way it goes. Listen, Honey, my friend Mary Louise will be along shortly. She has found the most divine little shop. Why don't you get dressed and come along?"

"Thanks a lot, but no! I want to go get a book."

"You mean you want to read it?"

"But, of course."

"Honey, I have never known you to be keen on reading before."

"True! But there comes a time in the life of every one. I just want to read about heather-clad hills and misty islands and peat fire flames and heroic deeds."

"I hope you don't mind me saying so, Charlotte, but I just hope Tom manages to set you on the right way when he gets here."

"I'm sure he will, Connie, I'm sure he will.

Tom looked at her across the table.

"This is all very sudden," he said.

"Yes, I'm sorry about the suddenness, but I'm not sorry about anything else."

"Was it acting on impulse?"

"No. It was from conviction."

"Well, thank God for conviction. What happened to us, Charlotte?"

"I don't know, Tom, and anyway that is of no importance now. What matters is what we are going to do with the rest of our lives."

He had called her from London and she was there to meet him at the airport. The day had become for them a voyage of discovery. It began as he came through the gate at the airport. He could scarcely believe that the casually elegant woman with the trace of makeup, the loose flowing hair, the flat shoes and the soft comfortable wool dress was his wife and yet she unmistakably was.

"Honey, you look just great."

He gave her the customary peck on the cheek so that he wouldn't disturb her makeup, although she appeared to be wearing very little. In turn, she gave him a robust hug and held on to him for a long time, quite oblivious to everything around her.

"Thank you, Sir. Compliments will get you everywhere. Come, let's have a coffee and then we'll find a cab."

She picked up one of the bags and made for the sliding door while he stood with mouth agape. He could not believe that Charlotte, the greatest stickler for what she called etiquette, and who always expected doors to be held open for her and someone to carry her bags, and a whole host of other 'standards to be kept', was now disappearing through the door with the heaviest of his bags in her hand.

"My God, she has changed … and how," he said to himself.

"What's happened to you, Charlotte?" he asked as the cab made its slow way into Edinburgh. "You are just so different. I sensed it when you called me the other night. I didn't realize just how much you have changed."

"Do you like it? Do you approve?"

"Do I ever like it? I can't begin to tell you."

"Then let us save it for later. We have a lot to talk about. We shall keep it for quieter moments. Meantime, you can tell me about your business deal. How did that go?"

"It went just swell. I took them all by surprise. I would happily have settled for a million less than I got. By the time Bob and that cartel realised what had happened, I had the whole thing sewn up and signed. They were all sore as Hell."

"Then you are not short of a dollar or two?"

"Quite the reverse. Whatever you want is yours, Babe. You can have the Ritz."

"I'm sorry, Tom. I don't ever want to appear ungrateful. I greatly appreciate your offer but, in truth, the Ritz is the last thing I want."

She put her arm round him and held him tight.

"I have everything I shall ever want right here."

"Not even a mink?"

"Not ever a mink."

"Then tell me what you would like."

"I'd like to show you Scotland. Not the tourist Scotland. There is a wonderful Scotland just off the highways. I'd like to show you that."

"And I would love to see it."

"It will take maybe three or four weeks."

"That's O.K. Thanks to my wife I am now out of a job, and besides I have a million or ten to spend."

Chapter Eight

It was nearly lunchtime when they arrived back at the hotel. When they got to the room, she sat him down in a comfortable chair. She went over to a sideboard and poured a generous Scotch for him. She added only a drop of water and two cubes of ice.

"Here, relax with this."

"I really should unpack."

"Have your drink. I shall unpack for you."

"But, Honey, you have never in your life ... "

She stood over him with her hands on her hips.

"Quit arguing and enjoy your drink or I'll tan your hide for you."

"Yes Ma'am, sure Ma'am."

She kissed his forehead.

"I just want to spoil you. May I?"

"Sure, Ma'am. The prospect of being spoiled by you is the most appealing I could ever imagine."

"I don't mean for just today ... I mean for the rest of your life."

"I'll drink to that any day. You know I don't know what I've done to deserve it, but all of a sudden my life looks rather wonderful and I'd like to spoil you in return."

She closed her eyes.

"Yes please," she whispered.

She surveyed the suits he had brought as she hung them in the closet.

"Hmm. A little formal for what I had in mind," she said.

"Gee, I'm sorry. If I had known I'd have packed my jeans."

"That wouldn't have been a bad idea. We can get you a couple of pairs tomorrow."

"You know, I believe you mean that."

"Yes I do. I mean ever word of it."

"But, Honey, you used to fuss if I even wore jeans in the house back in Beaumont."

She came and sat at his feet, taking his hands in hers.

"Tom, I have done a whole lot of things in the past, which I now know to be wrong. I had just chosen the wrong set of values. I am sorry as I can be and I shall get around to telling you how sorry I am for all the wrong things I have done to you, but that will take time. It will take a lot of time. I have a lot to make up to you and I shall get around to it. Meantime, I'll make a deal with you. Just accept what I do and if I do anything which goes against the grain just tell me and I shall quit it and, that apart, just sit back and enjoy what comes."

Over lunch he enlarged on the deal he had just pulled off.

"Clever Tom. You know you really are a smart man."

"Yes. We can loaf for the rest of our lives now."

"Is that what you want, Tom?"

"I don't quite know. I thought it might be what you would want."

"Thank you for thinking of me. You always did, but I think it is time we did what you would like. Have you any ideas what you would like to do?"

"I thought about things coming over in the plane. I have this feeling that I have burned my boats and that whatever I do will be something completely new."

"Like what?"

"I don't quite know. Leastwise not enough to come out and say what right now."

" I have an idea I'd like to put to you sometime. I think maybe you will like it."

"I'm sure I shall. Go ahead."

"No, not now. It will keep."

When they got back to their room she turned down the bedcover.

"You must be suffering from all kinds of jetlag, Honey. Why don't you take a nap? You will feel better after it."

"Do you have something in mind that you would like to do?"

"Yes, I have."

For a moment he was crestfallen and then he smiled.

"Sure, Honey, you go ahead."

She smiled. From somewhere a voice came to her: "Rely on your instincts. It is all there and what is there is good."

She busied herself as he undressed.

"Honey, did you see my pajamas when you unpacked? I can't seem to find them."

"No, I didn't see any pajamas. You must have forgotten to pack them."

"Gee, I'm sure I packed them. I am almost certain I did."

"Does it matter? It isn't that cold."

"But you never liked me to sleep in the raw."

"Tom, there is a whole lot of things I didn't like. I can't imagine why I didn't like them. Right now I can't see a thing wrong with sleeping in the raw."

"Then you don't mind?"

"Not in the slightest."

She had forgotten how good he looked. He had kept fit with hard physical work and with swimming and tennis. His hair was beginning to go gray at the temples and there was just a suggestion of thickening at the waist, but he was still a handsome and robust man. He slipped between the sheets and she bent and kissed him gently.

"Enjoy your afternoon, Babe," he said.

"I shall. I'm sure I shall."

She drew the curtains and turned the bedside lamp down to dim. She moved round to the other side of the bed and slowly began to undress. He stared in silent fascination as she removed every last article of clothing, and still he stared in silence. Never in all their married life had he seen her completely naked. She was beautiful, utterly beautiful. He sat up and leaned on one elbow as she slipped between the sheets.

"Doesn't a girl rate a kiss at least?"

"A girl rates something much more than a kiss," he said as he took her in his arms.

Later, she leaned over him and stroked his face and shoulders, his chest and down his belly.

"Sleep now, my love."

"I wouldn't dare."

"Why not?"

"I'm afraid to. I can't believe my good fortune. I'm afraid that it might go away if I go to sleep."

"It will never go away. Not unless you send it away."

"I shall never do that."

"I hope not. I sincerely hope not."

"Let's stop here, Honey," said Tom. "I'm about famished."

The village of Dunsyre nestles in a broad, wooded valley somewhere north of the city of Stirling. The sun was shining and there was a welcoming little inn just off the road. Tom drew up the car in front of it. The landlord was a fierce-looking man with a bushy red beard and wearing a kilt. His voice was surprisingly gentle for such a big man. He bade them welcome and brought them the menu as they had a drink.

"The salmon is very fresh," he commented. "It was caught just today."

The voice had a soft Highland lilt to it. That and the sight of the kilt brought all kinds of memories flooding back to Charlotte. She was thankful that Tom and the landlord were deep in conversation. It gave her a moment to sort out her thoughts. Tom turned to her to ask what she would like. They both settled for the poached fresh salmon. The sweet was soft lush local raspberries liberally doused with cream.

"Were the raspberries caught today too?" asked Tom.

"The raspberries were picked yesterday."

They sat back and discussed what they would do now as they had their coffee.

"You will no doubt like a wee drop of whisky with your coffee," said Lachie. They were now on first name terms.

"Sounds a great idea, but I think I'd better pass," said Tom. "I'm driving, you know."

"And where would you be driving to?" asked Lachie.

"I don't rightly know. We thought we might drive on till we find someplace."

"And what is wrong with this place? Don't you like it? This is not a hotel as such, but we do have two or three guest rooms."

He sounded just a little peeved.

"And you could give us a room for the night?"

"You will be most welcome."

"Then I guess we would like a wee drop of whisky with our coffee."

Lachie went off to arrange the room for them.

"I can see why you are taken with the Highlands, Honey. You know, what I like most about this place is that there is no television, not a slot machine in sight and no pool tables."

"Yes, and you will soon find many other attractive aspects of the Highlands. Not least of these is their laid-back attitude to life. It isn't indolence. It is more of a philosophy. Somehow they have retained many of the basic things, which make life worthwhile. They have the time and take the time to talk. It is a simple lifestyle. I think it is a lovely one."

"I kind of agree with you. It has certainly worked some magic with you."

"It has indeed."

On their first afternoon together, she awoke before he did. She lay holding his hand and she pondered what she should do. She could not put off for much longer telling him of the reasons for the change in her life. She wondered if she should tell Tom of her time with Hector.

"I may do some time. I shall not do so just now."

Hector had been right. She did not love Tom and her children any less for that experience. She loved them more. Her time with Tom was now a time of happiness and contentment. They felt easy and comfortable with each another.

"No," she decided, "I can't let go of this. What we have now is something precious. I cannot risk losing it just yet. I shall tell him what I have learned from my Highland fling. I shall not tell him all the circumstances, not yet."

"That is an old Scots pine," said Tom, as they wandered through the old forest. "At one time most of the Highlands were covered by the old Caledonian forest and it was made up largely of such trees."

"You have come a long way in just four days. I declare you are now at the stage of teaching Lachie something of his native history." Charlotte smiled as she teased him. They fell in love with Dunsyre. They left the car by the inn and they walked through woods and over heather-clad hills and they took time to talk to the people in the village and sometimes they just sat and read books. It was enough that they were near to each other.

Tom read avidly about the ancient Scots.

"They were, in many ways, a bloodthirsty lot," was his comment. "After a violent history like that, they can stand a bit of peace and quiet. Little wonder they treasure their peaceful life."

Charlotte expressed surprise at his interest.

"Oh, it has always been there. I just never have had the time to indulge myself."

She had difficulty in persuading Tom to move on. Lachie had breakfast with them every morning. Breakfast sometimes lasted for nearly two hours. Like many of his Highland race, Lachie was a born storyteller. They sat enthralled as he told them of the history and customs and way of life of the Highlander. And he told them of the Hebrides where they still spoke Gaelic and wove tweed.

"He makes it all sound so wonderful. You just have to want to see it all. We must go to some Highland Games too."

"Oh, I have been to a Highland Games. They tend to be a bit crowded."

She had dreaded this moment. It was too soon to meet Hector again.

"Still, I would like to see those big men in action," said Tom.

"Well, perhaps if we come across a smaller gathering," said Charlotte. She knew that the athletes, with whom Hector traveled, all attended the bigger gatherings.

They took the road west and they stopped to admire the shaggy Highland cattle with their big widespread horns mirrored in the calm waters of a loch. They arrived in Oban late one night. It was a bustling and busy town and they took the boat to Mull next morning. Charlotte thought it would be safe to attend the games there. Nether Lorne was just across the water. Hector would not be so near to home.

That was the day of the Mull Highland games. They walked from the hotel and up the hill to the golf course above Tobermory where the games were held. Tom was enthralled. The Highland dancers delighted him and the heavyweight athletes left him full of admiration as they threw the hammer and tossed the caber and wrestled and threw heavy stones over a bar high above their heads. They met some of the athletes in the beer tent during the games. Tom told them how impressed he was and just how much he was enjoying the games.

"Oh, we are the small fry," they said. "We're not a patch on Hunter or MacIver or the rising young star, Hector Maclean."

Charlotte's heart missed a beat at the mention of his name.

They took a ferry to the Outer Hebrides. They made slow progress. Charlotte had made out a schedule, which would allow them to see most of the Highlands and Islands, but often Tom would fall in love with a place and she could not get him to move on. Very soon she gave up. It was not a hard decision to take.

Chapter Nine

They were delighted with the Uists, but Barra completely captivated them. This tiny island, with its empty golden beaches, sandy grasslands, abundance of wild flowers and rugged interior soon had Tom in its spell. Not for nothing is it called Barradise. It was here that they filmed the movie 'Whisky Galore', better known in the States as 'Tight Little Island'. They stayed in Castlebay, the main town on the island. It was little more than a village, which began as a nineteenth century fishing port. Today it is home to the vehicle ferry, which brings in much of the island's food and supplies. They found a delightful place to stay. Mrs MacNeil - what else on Barra? - Was a plump comfortable widow who had been born on the island and never once in her sixty years had seen any reason to leave it, not even for an hour?

"The best way to see this island is on foot or by bicycle," she advised.

They hired bicycles, but their first sightseeing was by boat.

"You had better start off with the castle," suggested Mrs. MacNeil. "I'll get Donald to take you over in his wee boat."

Kisimul Castle sits on a rocky islet in the bay just off Castlebay. Legend has it that this has been the stronghold of the MacNeils since the eleventh century. The castle, with its square keep and curtain wall, was built to withstand sieges. The castle was equipped with two artesian wells to provide water and a fish-trap in a catchments basin. A galley used to be berthed alongside on a sloping beach with the crew house nearby. At the first sign of trouble, the crew was expected to launch the ship and defend the castle from attack.

Charlotte and Tom felt some sort of kinship with Barra because of its strong connection with the States. The 21st chief had to sell Barra in 1838 and soon the castle was in ruins. Many of the MacNeils went to seek a better life in America. In the late 1930s, the 45th clan chief, an American architect, returned to the island and bought the castle. Before his death in 1970, he succeeded in completing the much-needed restoration work. Water was piped from Castlebay and telephones installed. His son Ian Roderick, Professor of Law, is the current Chief of the MacNeils of Barra. The Clan Gathering takes place every 10 years on Barra. Charlotte had great difficulty dragging Tom away. In the evening they climbed the high hill overlooking Castlebay. Halfway up the hill stood 'Our Lady of the Sea', a white marble statue of the Madonna and Child.

"Now, I think you had better start off with Vatersay," advised Mrs. MacNiel next morning.

Tom raised his eyebrows

"The wee island," she explained patiently.

The whole of Barra seemed steeped in history. This tiny island just south of Castlebay had a monument to victims of a shipwreck, which occurred in 1853 when the Annie Jane left Liverpool bound for Quebec with hundreds of emigrants. The ship was swept onto the rocky Vatersay coast and most of the passengers were drowned. There was also a beautiful sandy beach on the eastern side of the island. They had it entirely to themselves.

They took to their bicycles and followed the main road in a clockwise direction from Castlebay. They had their packed lunch at Macleod's Tower, Dun Mhic Leoid (a few miles west of Castlebay). It is also known as Castle Sinclair and it stood on an islet in Loch Tangusdale. It is a medieval tower-house with walls 1.4 metres thick. Nearby was the so-called St. Columba's Well.

On their journey they came across a small standing stone near the roadside and, following a dirt track, came to a museum in a thatched cottage. They walked almost a mile to Dun Bharpa, a large well-preserved Neolithic chambered burial cairn and then, on a low hill close to the road, found the well-preserved remains of an Iron Age broch. They smiled in amusement when they came to the nine-hole golf course at Grean with electrified fencing around the greens to keep the sheep away.

Next day they took the road leading up the Eoligarry peninsula. It was here they gazed in amazement at the Cockle Strand. This huge tidal beach serves as the island's airstrip for regular flights from Glasgow and Benbecula. It is unique in this country as being the only runway washed by the sea, and the flight times are decided according to the tides. The islanders go out collecting cockles from the wet sand.

'Suidheachan' is a huge white bungalow overlooking Cockle Strand. It was built for famous author Compton Mackenzie. He is buried in a very plain grave in Cille Bharra cemetery, a little way up the hillside overlooking Eoligarry jetty. Two twelfth-century chapels stand in the middle. One is in ruins, while the other has been restored to house carved stones and a sort of Catholic shrine.

"Let's have a drink before we go back, Honey," said Tom.

They had the bar to themselves. Tom had a pint, and Charlotte a shandy. They chatted to the two girls behind the bar.

"Och, yes. You are Mr. and Mrs. Benson, the couple who are staying with Mrs. MacNeil," said one of the girls.

It didn't surprise them in any way. In four days they had come to know most of the islanders and the whole island seemed to know them.

"Mrs. MacNeil is my aunt," explained Cathy. "You'll be going to the ceilidh tonight?" she added.

"We hadn't given it any thought."

"Have you ever been to a ceilidh before?"

"No, I can't say that I have."

"Then you must. It is an experience never to be missed."

"So what exactly happens at a ceilidh?"

"Och, just the usual things; there's music and singing and dancing and everyone must join in and of course there's a good dram as well to make things go with a swing."

"Oh, I don't know," said Charlotte. "You see, neither of us has ever done any Scottish dancing. We'd probably make first class fools of ourselves."

"Think nothing of it. You'll manage fine," said Rhona.

"It could well be embarrassing."

"Not at all. Look, Cathy and I will teach you a few of the basic steps right now. That and the whisky will be enough to see you through the evening."

Over the next half-hour, with a great deal of laughter, the girls taught Charlotte and Tom the basics of pas de bas and the sequences of the reels and jigs. They decided after five minutes that Charlotte was a natural, and at the end of half-an-hour declared Tom "quite sufficiently accomplished in the art of country dancing to tackle any ceilidh".

"We'll see you tonight," they called as Tom and Charlotte left the pub.

"I can't help thinking we are getting in over our depth," said Charlotte.

"Oh let's give it a try, anyway," said Tom. "It could just turn out to be fun.

Mrs. MacNeil sat between them. The room looked quite Spartan, but the atmosphere was warm and welcoming. They listened to the Gaelic songs, which they found strange at first, but then the wistful lonely quality of the sad airs became familiar and they found themselves strangely touched. In between times, they danced and drank whisky. Cathy and Rhona were eager to show off the prowess of their pupils. At the outset Rhona had brought them an outsize measure of whiskey.

"That will calm any nerves you might have," she said philosophically.

Charlotte and Tom were not afforded the chance to sit out a single dance. Charlotte could not quite decide whether the rosy glow on Tom's cheeks was due to the exertion or to the whisky.

"Probably a bit of both," she decided. She herself was beginning to feel very mellow indeed.

At the end of a reel she noticed that Tom had disappeared.

"Have you seen Tom?" she asked Mrs. MacNeil. "He is not in the hall."

"Och, yes. He's just gone out for a wee while. Don't worry, he's fine. He'll be back presently."

Charlotte was not convinced. She began to worry a little after five minutes, but she didn't want to show it. There was a roll of drums and Cathy and Rhona appeared with Tom between them. He was resplendent in kilt and sporran.

"God! He looks just great," thought Charlotte.

"We'll have a dashing white sergeant, thank you Mr. M.C., and Tom is going to be our partner."

Tom got a great cheer when the dance finished. He returned to Charlotte looking very rosy and happy.

"I'm greatly impressed," whispered Charlotte.

"You'll have to check that he is properly dressed," whispered Cathy to Charlotte.

"How do I do that?"

"You just slip your hand up his kilt," she laughed.

"I'll leave that for later, I think."

"I'm sure you won't be disappointed," she said mischievously.

"There's only one thing wrong with islands like Barra," said Tom as they boarded the ferry.

"What's that?" said Charlotte.

"You get such a pang of regret when you finally have to leave them," he answered.

They stood in silent awe on the island of Harris, as they watched the sun set. The sea changed by the minute from blood red through pinks to molten gold and then through silver and blue. They saw the women make the tweed and all the while they sang old Gaelic songs, and they watched fascinated as an old woman made the soft material into a garment on an ancient sewing machine. The belt from the treadle had long gone and it had been replaced with knicker elastic. The garment was beautifully made.

They then crossed back to Skye. They were two lovers walking hand in hand through wonderland.

"I could stay here forever," remarked Tom as they sat high on the side of the Cuillins, the rugged mountains that form the backbone of the Isle of Skye. The heather on the hills was now in full bloom and the slopes around them were a tableau of subtle colour. Even the sounds around them were understated.

"I don't want to spoil your dream, but we do have three kids back in the States."

"Gee, yes. I had almost forgotten."

"Have you thought about what you want to do?"

"No. The world of oil wells and big deals no longer holds any attraction for me. After this I think I shall need something nearer to nature."

"What about a ranch?"

"A ranch would be just great, but you would never live on a ranch."

"Try me."

"Honey, you have never been on a ranch. It would be like living on Mars."

"Why should it? I had never traveled in the Highlands before either and I just love it."

"Wouldn't you miss the Beaumont society life?"

"Even less than you would miss your oil wells. Tom, let's try it. If it doesn't work out we can always sell out and try something else."

"Honey, you got a deal. There is nothing I would like to do more."

She felt the firm clasp of his hand on hers. They were friends. They were lovers. It was almost four weeks since he had arrived and in that time they had grown even closer. In the first week or so they felt they had to work at their new relationship. Now it was natural and something very dear to both of them and the days slipped past almost unnoticed. Only very rarely now did they remember the turmoil and the tensions of their former lives.

The boat rocked gently on the waves. Tom put down his book and stretched luxuriously.

"God! This life gets to you."

"The last thing I want to do is spoil your pleasure, but it did cross my mind that the boys return from summer camp in two weeks. We really should be there when they get home."

He sighed. "Yes, I suppose it is too good to last for ever. How much longer can we stay?"

"A week. Ten days at the most."

"There are two things I really want to do before I go."

"Sure, Honey. Then let's do them."

"Well, I would like to spend two or three days with Lachie and Morag and I would like to go to Braemar Highland games."

"I agree with Dunsyre, but do you want to go to Braemar?"

"Heck, yes. We have seen two of the smaller gatherings. I would like to see a big gathering just once, and they don't come bigger or better than Braemar."

Never in all of her life had there been a month like the one they had just had, but way down deep there had been a secret dread and now it had come to the surface. It was time to face up to the inevitable.

"Whatever happens now," she thought, "no one can ever take these four weeks away from me."

Tom had shipped the oars and thrown two baited lines overboard, but even the trout were too lazy to bite. She spoke in a small voice.

"Tom, I can't go to Braemar. There is a special reason why I can't go there. Tom, I have a confession to make, but before I do, I want you to know that I love you more than I have ever done. I love you more than anything else in all of this world. You may want to send me away when I have told you - I shall understand. It will break my heart, but I shall understand."

The tears flowed down her cheeks.

"Charlotte, what is it? What's the matter?"

"No, Tom, let me talk. When I left Connie at Loch Lomond, I did not go off on my own for five days as I told you. I went off with some one."

Through the tears and sobs she told him of her meeting with Hector and of their days together. She left nothing out. When she had finished she let her head fall to her knees and her shoulders shook with sobs. She felt a hand gently stroke her neck. After a little he took her face between his hands. He looked into her eyes and then he bent and kissed her gently on the lips. He sat beside her and his arms felt strong and comforting.

"Oh, Tom, I am sorry. I am just so sorry."

"Were you in love with him?"

"No. There was never any question of being in love. You see I had had time to think. I knew that all the time and effort I had spent over the last few years meant very little. My world was in ruins. I was just kind of lost. Hector was lost too in a way."

"Tom, there are traditions in the Highlands, of which we might not wholly approve, but they are there and they still adhere to them in the more remote areas. Hector fell foul of those traditions. He fell in love at an early age. Despite their Presbyterian upbringing, he and his girl made love. They made love very frequently and soon Bessie, that is the girl's name, was pregnant. That was where they fell foul of the traditions. Hector was sent to an aunt in Glasgow to finish his studies. Bessie was sent to Edinburgh to have their child and finish her studies. Hector's parents are bringing up the child. Hector has never seen his son. They are not supposed to ever be in contact, but they are. They were willing to go along so far with the traditions, but they are determined to be together one day soon."

"What a tragic love affair. Little wonder he was a bit lost."

"Yes, but he was so mature, they both were. He is strong in both mind and body. He has the guts to make it, but I think he hurt a lot inside. Tom, he is not yet nineteen."

"Oh, my God!"

"We were like two orphans in a storm. We comforted each other. It was nothing more than that. Tom I was never in love with him, but I cannot help but be grateful to him. He was young, but he was so mature. Some of that maturity brushed off on me. I could never have got to this stage without him. I have to be grateful to him."

"Then I think I should be grateful to him too. Oh, Babe, you've had it tough."

"Yes, it was tough, but I made it. I think I am a better person for it. Will you send me away from you?"

"Why should I send you away?"

"Tom, I have been unfaithful to you."

He drew her on to his knee and he held her close.

"Honey," he said in a low voice, "the day I arrived you told me that what happened before was of no importance. I happen to think that is still true. If it is any consolation, I have been unfaithful to you too on a few occasions. Somehow we were each responsible for the actions of the other. I went elsewhere to get the kind of loving I could not get at home. You went elsewhere because I was too tied up with my work to notice that you needed me. Honey, that is all in the past. It is in the past for both of us. These last four weeks have been far and away the best ever in my life. I think they have been good for you too."

"Oh, Tom, yes. They have been far and away the best in my life too."

"Then we would be crazy to throw away what we have found. I'll make a deal with you. We leave all our troubles out here in the water and when we get to the shore we start anew. We shall go for the kind of life we have been talking about this last month. Agreed?"

"Agreed. Oh, Tom, I love you."

"I love you too, Babe."

There was a fish on one of the lines.

"Oh Tom, let it go. We shouldn't kill anything on a day like this."

"No, we shouldn't, should we?"

He eased the hook from its jaw and gently put it back in the water.

"Sorry, and have a nice day," he called to it as it swam away.

Chapter Ten

The car had barely stopped and Lachie was opening the door for her. He enveloped her in a huge bear hug. The smell of pipe tobacco from his waistcoat brought back to Charlotte just how much she had come to treasure this man. They were welcomed back like returning prodigals.

"Come away in. I shall get tea and then you must tell me all about your travels."

Morag brought feather-light scones hot from the oven. She served them with homemade raspberry jam and fresh cream. Over tea they described how they had wandered through the Highlands and Islands.

"That is just the way to travel," said Lachie. "You must never hurry through our country. You will miss so much if you hurry. Now off with you and have your baths. We have a haunch of venison just waiting for such an occasion as this. We shall have a good dram before dinner."

"Oh, Tom, I feel like I have come home," she said when they got to their room.

"I know what you mean. I could live here for ever."

"It would be nice," she said dreamily. "You know, Tom, I have been thinking. We don't really have a home now."

"What about the house in Beaumont?"

"Yes, I know. It is our house. It is not our home. We lived there because of your work. You don't work there any more. Tom, we shall have to find a home, a real home."

"Yes, Babe. We'll get to work on it when we get back to the States."

He began to sing 'My Heart's in the Highlands'.

Charlotte stole a glance at Tom and she smiled. Who was this eloquent romantic man? The Highland magic had worked its spell on Tom too.

"I hope it never wears off," she thought.

Lachie poured generous whiskies and sat back.

"Och, it is so good to have you back," he said. "We've missed you while you have been away."

"Yes," said Tom, "and it is just great to be back. We said there were two things we had to do before we returned to the States. One was to spend a day or two with you and the other was to attend the Braemar Games."

"Tom," he said, "you are right. You can't go back to the States without seeing one of the big Highland gatherings."

They were sitting back replete after a wonderful dinner. Morag was sure that they had been undernourished for the past four weeks. She was intent on making amends.

Lachie sat back, and for the next hour he regaled them with stories of the delights of past Highland Games he had seen.

"What are the origins of Highland Games? Does anyone know or are they just lost in the mists of time."

"No! We do know quite a bit about the origins."

"According to tradition, Scottish Highland games had their beginning when originated by the kings and chiefs of Scotland as a reasonable method of choosing the best men at arms. Crude forms of the athletic events you see today were developed to test the contestants for strength, stamina, accuracy and agility.

Of course, they used the elements and materials of their day-to-day life and so the caber toss, archery, wrestling, and foot races up steep hills were seen. Even Highland dancing was used to tax the endurance and strength of competitors. You see, even the Scottish regiments used to require Highland dancing as a form of training to develop stamina and agility.

"The present-day popularity of the Scottish Games must be credited to Queen Victoria, who developed a love for Scotland, its people and things Scottish early in her life. After the death of Prince Albert, she spent very long periods at Balmoral. She, with her entire Royal family, regularly attended the Scottish Highland Games held at Braemar."

"It is very easy to fall in love with the Highlands," said Tom.

"Well, if stories are to be believed she fell in love with a particular lusty Highlander, too. It is said the Ghillie John Brown was tossing his caber in that direction on a very regular basis."

"Now, Lachie!" Said Morag crossly.

"Och, sorry Morag," said Lachie, "but the present-day Royal Family are no less enthusiastic about the games and come the first week-end of September. They will be well represented at the Games."

"As if the spectacle on its own was not enough, it is steeped in history too, like most of the very good things about Scotland."

"Yes, and the great thing about Highland games is that you can approach them on so many levels. At one end they are worth a visit for the sheer spectacle of the pipe bands and the dancers and the athletes, and, at the other, for the real aficionados there is the intricacy and finer points which most people miss completely.'

"I'll tell you what, I'll take you both to the Braemar Games this week-end. All of the big names will be there, Hunter and MacIver and young Maclean. Ah, what a bonnie athlete that boy is. Yes that is just what we shall do."

Charlotte had a choking feeling. A feeling of dread came over her. She felt Tom's eyes on her. She lowered her eyes and gazed into the peat fire.

"That sounds swell, Lachie," said Tom. "I would love to go to Breamar. I don't know about Charlotte, though. We've done a lot of traveling these past four weeks. I really think she should rest up for a day or two before we go back to the States and, besides, she has seen the big names before I got here."

She felt immense gratitude welling up within her. How understanding Tom was. At that moment she loved him more than ever. He really was some one very special.

"Yes, I think she should take things easy for a day or two," said Morag. "Why don't the two of you go off to Braemar and leave Charlotte and me here. You will feel much more free without us."

"Then that's what we shall do. We shall take young Hamish with us to do the driving, so that we can have a dram, and we might manage a spot of fishing in the Tay or on the Clunie while we are there."

Tom raised his eyebrows

"The Clunie is a fine trout stream just by Braemar," explained Lachie.

She walked in the old forest. It had been there for hundreds of years. There was a comforting permanence about the trees. There was a mellow mistiness to the days and they were now crisp at the edges. The woods were a riot of yellow and russet. The autumn clad leaves of the silver birch looked like a lemon yellow snow-flurry. Charlotte missed Tom, but she was glad of the solitude. She needed the time to reflect and contemplate. She pondered long on the future.

"Why is it," she wondered, "that we take so long to find ourselves? Why should it have taken so much time and a young Highlander for me to discover my real sexuality and the pleasure it now brings me? We are too conditioned by our upbringing. It never occurred to me to question what I was being taught when young, and yet I should have. I should never have allowed my early circumstances to condition my married life to such an extent. How much time we have lost? We must lose no more."

She was sure that Tom would meet Hector. She was only a little concerned about the outcome. With her maturity came a confidence and a trust in life, which had not been there before.

Chapter Eleven

It seemed that one frame of spectacular scenery followed closely on the heels of another and each seemed grander than the one before. Tom was so transfixed by the passing scenery that he could barely speak to Lachie. After many detours, for all manner of reasons, they were now nearing their destination.

Braemar is a large village located at 1000 feet near the junction of the Clunie River with the River Dee. Historically, it was strategically placed in the best position for controlling the great valleys and mountain passes that head to the east, west and south. For nearly a thousand years, the castles of Kindrochit and Braemar have played a central role in Scottish history. In the present-day, however, the stresses and strains of modern life having largely by-passed Braemar, its importance is as a base for visitors wishing to explore those hills and valleys or to relax by skiing, fishing or simply enjoying the surroundings.

When she visited in 1845, the beauty of Deeside, the quality of the air and the good climate captivated Queen Victoria. She and Prince Albert then bought and rebuilt Balmoral Castle. Since then the Royal Family have regularly holidayed at Balmoral and frequently visited Braemar. The climate is good in summer and autumn. Indeed, when displaying autumn colours, the road between Braemar and Crathie past Balmoral is perhaps the most beautiful in Britain. Conditions can be severe in winter and bracing in the spring - not surprising when Glenshee, Scotland's largest ski center, is only eight miles away. The tops of the high Cairngorms, which can be seen from various points in the village, often carry snow into early summer.

Lachie kept Tom well informed. He pointed out to the numerous beauty spots and castles, which they passed as they neared Braemar. Braemar Castle is only one mile east of the village and Balmoral Castle only eight miles further on.

"They seem plentifully supplied with castles in these parts," said Tom.

"Och, yes, and there are plenty other nearby castles like Corgarff, Craigievar, Drum and Crathes; and, of course, close by Balmoral is the Royal Lochnagar Distillery too."

Tom was amused by the trail tours, which were on offer. There were 'The Victorian Heritage Trail', 'The Malt Whisky Trail' and 'The Castle Trail'. And also the beauty spots like Loch Muick, Muir of Dinnet and Mar Lodge Estate, and gems such as the Linn of Dee, the Linn of Quoich and the 'Auld Brig o' Dee'.

"This is an experience not to be missed," Tom thought to himself. "You can't find too many places like this today. It is remote. There are no crowded motorways to get you uptight. There is only this sense of complete relaxation."

Lachie's voice intruded into his reverie at that point.

"Now, Tom," he said, "would you like to approach these games as a tourist or would you like to approach them on a more serious level?"

"I think the latter, Lachie."

"If you are to get the best out of your visit to the games, you should know something about them. Would you like me to give you some background?"

"Of course, I would."

"Well, I'll try not to be too boring."

"Fat chance of that Lachie," thought Tom.

"Now the Scottish Heavy Events have been a part of Highland Games for centuries. The ancient Heavy Events date back early in Scottish history, originating during the reign of King Malcolm Canmore. The games consisted of seven traditional events. They were held over two days. At the end of the second day of competition, all the points are totaled, the winner being the one with the most points. Nowadays you get all sorts of variations. That has more to do with the tourist trade and not a few of the heavy athletes who are not the men they used to be."

"They are all pretty good specimens of manhood from what I have seen," said Tom.

"Ah, but not what they once were. They tend to take the easy and more profitable road rather than follow the more pure forms that once were followed. There are a few who would prefer to stick to the purely traditional ways. Young Hector Maclean for one. I have only met him a few times, but what a mature young man he is, an old head on young shoulders, and a great athlete as well. If I get the chance I shall introduce him. He is one athlete I really admire."

"I hope you do get the chance, Lachie. I have never met the man, but I think I greatly admire him too," thought Tom.

"But all that is by the way," said Lachie. "We are stuck with attracting the tourists to keep up the games and for that we must go along the commercial route, but I'll tell you what used to be. Most of the events are still there anyway. The basic events are the ancient stone-throw, the first event of the competition. It resembles the modern day shot-put event, but a twenty-two to twenty-four pound stone picked from the local river is used.

"Next comes the fifty-six pound heavy weight throw. The weight is thrown with one hand for horizontal distance. Scoring is identical to that of the stone-throw. Next comes the twenty-two pound ancient hammer. The athlete has his back facing in the direction of the throw. He is not permitted to spin. He whirls the hammer around his head as fast as possible, releasing it at its maximum speed. Scoring is similar to that of the stone-throw.

"Now, the caber toss, which comes next, was always done over two days. The caber toss is considered the most impressive of the heavy events. The caber is generally a spruce log measuring about twenty feet and weighing approximately a hundred and twenty pounds. The athlete shoulders the caber, cupping the small end in his two hands. Once the caber is balanced, the athlete runs and releases it by heaving it so that it goes end over end. Those who successfully turn the caber in this fashion, continue on to compete in the Challenge Caber on day two. A caber that fails to flip is not recorded.

"To round off day one, there is the hay toss. This is always the last event of day one. Pole vault standards are set up. The athletes attempt to throw a sixteen to eighteen pound bag of hay up and over the bar on the standards. The athletes use a pitchfork to toss the bag of hay.

"You will appreciate that it takes quite some stamina to complete that programme, but even more is needed on day two. First off they have to tackle the Twenty Six Pound Weight Toss for Distance. This event starts off the second day of competition and then comes the sixteen-pound ancient hammer. This event is executed in the same way as the twenty-two pound hammer that is tossed on day one.

"Then, to really separate the men from the boys, there is the fifty-six pound Weight for Height. In this backbreaking event, the athlete tosses the weight described in the heavy weight throw over the pole vault bar. The weight is tossed with one hand only and the athlete is allowed only three tries at any given height.

Then comes the Final Caber event. The rules for this are the same as for day one, but just to make sure the athletes are not getting soft, the caber used on the second day is usually longer - twenty feet - and heavier, at fifty pounds. And finally there is the Farmers' Walk.

"This event is a real crowd-pleaser, as spectators are allowed to participate. The competitor stands between two suitcase-like weights each weighing three hundred pounds or more. All the competitor has to do is grasp the handles on the weights and then walk with them as far as he is able.

"The athletes are scored for every event except for the Hay Toss and the Farmers' Walk, as they are not traditional events. The points are awarded according to where the athlete places in each event. These points are totaled, the winner being the one with the most points."

"That is one hell of a program. I shan't remember all of that, but I'm impressed as hell."

"Don't worry, Tom, I'll keep you updated at every stage. You'll be all right."

"Thanks, I'm sure I shall."

"Is it always this crowded?" asked Tom as they settled in their seats in the stand.

"This and then some," commented Lachie. "Booking starts in the first week of February and you couldn't get a seat in this stand for love nor money after the end of February."

"Which leaves me wondering how you managed to secure two of the best seats so late in the day."

"Well, I'm afraid I must just leave you to wonder, dear Tom."

"And that's the end of that particular conversation," thought Tom.

There was a buzz of excitement as the Royal party arrived.

"My God, they look quite ordinary," was Tom's first reaction. He had only ever seen them in newspapers or on films. They could have been any family out for the day. The formalities and greeting were kept as low-key as possible. Not even the Royal Family was allowed to overshadow the spectacle and grandeur of the proceedings.

It was above all a feast for the eyes. Tom could hardly tear his eyes away from the dancers and the marching pipe bands, but his real interest was in the heavyweight events. His heart missed a beat when he heard the name of Hector Maclean and the spectacular young man stepped forward to throw the hammer. His muscles knotted and the dark auburn hair gleamed in the autumn sunlight as he sent the hammer skyward. Although he appeared much younger than the other competitors, he was not overawed by the occasion.

"Now that is a magnificent throw," said Lachie with admiration.

Tom grunted in assent. He hoped that his face did not betray his emotions. He had wondered how he would react to seeing Hector for the first time. He had not counted on such outright admiration.

"So this is Hector, and who wouldn't admire Hector? He quite puts the rest in the shade and that is no mean feat in this company. But it isn't just looks. I am aware of that more than perhaps anyone else at this gathering. I know of your maturity, Hector. I know of how you face up to your commitments, and of your compassion and concern for others, and I am aware, above all, of how much in your debt I am now, and always will be. Although you are not aware of it, you saved my marriage for me and, I think, set Charlotte and me on the road to a much more rewarding lifestyle. I hope I get the chance to shake your hand, Hector."

He was aware that Lachie was addressing him.

"You are away in the clouds, Tom. Is the Celtic twilight getting to you?"

"Looks so, Lachie. What was it you were saying?"

"I was just making a suggestion that after the games are over we shall take ourselves over to the Brig."

"I'm game. What exactly is the Brig?"

"Oh, it is a hostelry to which quite a few of the heavyweight athletes proceed after the games for a dram and a bit of socialising. We might be in luck and meet a few of them face to face."

"Great, Lachie."

"That was certainly one of the highlights of my life. I shall be thinking of this day many years from now, Lachie. I just can't find words to thank you."

"My pleasure, Tom. It is just fine to have some one who is interested, not just in the spectacle, but in the finer points too."

They were making their way towards the Brig. Hamish had to drive at a crawling pace down the road. It gave plenty of time for reminiscing.

"You know, as the competitions were taking place I couldn't help putting them in the context of preparation for battle, the battles which they fought in the Highlands against the English and against each other. And all of the factions and loyalties and disloyalties that were so rife in the Highland past," said Tom

"I wouldn't be too impressed, Tom. I wouldn't want you to go away with the wrong impression. You see, most of those battles which the tourist brochures make such a big deal of, well, the truth is that most of them were badly fought and quite unnecessary in the first place."

"Perhaps you are right, Lachie, but the same could be said for almost any battle in almost any conflict. If you don't mind, I'll hang on to the romance. It is a compelling romance that I am having with the Highlands."

"Then the last thing I would like is to spoil it for you."

"It will be whisky?"

"Is that a question?"

"Let's say a strong suggestion."

One of the big men at the bar turned towards them then.

"Oh, it's Lachie," he said. He grabbed Lachie's hand in his great paw and pumped it vigorously.

"Well, and we haven't seen much of you this year. Have you gone off the Highland Games or what?"

"No, I'd never go off Highland Games, but all sorts of things have got in the way this year. I did manage Cowal and Blairgowrie though."

"Well done. Anyway, you'll have a dram. What will it be?"

"Now, I was just about to get my friend Tom here a Lochnagar. By the way, let me introduce Tom. He's from the States. I'm introducing him to the Highland Games. Tom, meet Charles and Alan Maclean."

Tom looked up to the two big men. They both stood well over six feet and were as broad as barn doors. They were very similar in appearance. They had curling black hair; luxurious mustaches and smiling mischievous blue blue eyes, and Tom took an instant liking to them. They shook his hand warmly and bade him welcome to the Highlands. They were gentle as kittens.

"You are in good hands, Tom," said Charles. "Lachie knows just about as much as anyone about the finer points of the Highland Games."

"We are about to go on to lesson two," said Lachie. " I have to show him something of our whisky traditions too."

"I'm sure you will be up to the task, Lachie, but let's start him off on the right road. Large Lochnagars it will be. I always think it etiquette to start off with the local whisky where ever you are in the Highlands," said Alan.

Tom had a momentary trepidation as they all drank his health.

"I wonder if I shall be up to the task," he thought inwardly.

"Och, look! Here's our bairn. It is Hector himself," said Alan.

"You did well, my wee boy," said Charles, slapping Hector warmly on the back.

"That first throw was just two inches short of the national record. You'll get there very soon."

"Next year, without a doubt," said Lachie. "Congratulations, Hector, and you did very well in the other events as well. It was great to see you beat Andy Campbell in the heavy stone. He has hogged that event to himself for too long. I think Andy is a bit sore about that. He's threatening revenge next year."

"And he might just get it," said Hector. "Nice to see you again, Lachie."

"And great to see you. Meet my fried Tom from the States. He is on holiday. He's just been on a trip round the Highlands and he couldn't go back without seeing Braemar."

"Pleased to meet you, Tom. I hope you enjoyed your trip."

The brothers caught his attention at that point.

"Will you have a dram, Hecky?"

"No thanks. I'll stick with apple juice."

"Och, come on, you are a big boy now. A wee dram will not harm you."

"I know it will not harm me. I've had a dram before now, but I'll stick with apple juice. I'm driving."

"Oh, all right old sober sides."

"Some one in our family has to be a bit sober and it certainly isn't going to be you two."

"You are damned right there, Hecky boy. You're damned right there. There are far too many miserable buggers in this life without our adding to their number."

"Meaning me?"

"No, not meaning you, Hecky boy. You are serious, maybe a bit too serious at times, but you are never miserable."

"Well, thanks for that much. How are things at home? How are mother and father? I haven't heard recently."

"Everyone is just fine, and the wee boy is coming on just great. A true Maclean, he has a great mop of black hair already and the eyes are blue as the ocean. Everyone just dotes on him."

"I'm very glad to hear that."

He turned to Tom.

"Sorry, Tom, you were saying you had been on a trip through the Highlands and Islands. I hope you enjoyed it."

"Oh, immensely! We were fortunate to meet Lachie on the first day of our trip. He roused our interest and it snowballed from there. I would not have missed the past few weeks for anything in the world."

"Did you attend any other Highland Games?"

"Yes we got our first taste in Mull and that was us hooked."

"Ah, yes. That is a fine venue to start with. It is a lovely setting up there on the golf course. Did you see much of the Highlands?"

"Quite a bit. We traveled through the Outer Hebrides and then back to Skye. The trouble was tearing ourselves away from a place. Everywhere had its own charm and interest and we just ran out of time. What a wonderful lifestyle they have in the Highlands. We felt quite privileged to be a part of it."

Hector smiled.

"It does seem to have made quite an impression on you."

"Didn't it ever? You know, Hector, it isn't just the natural beauty. That is there and gets to you very quickly, but what is also there is a lovely lifestyle. It still has all the things that are really important in life. It is something approaching a philosophy. I was quite captivated."

"I think you have discovered the essence of the Highlands, Tom. Not everyone does."

"I think it means a lot to you, Hector."

"Yes, and I get quite fearful for the future of the Highlands at times."

"How is that?"

"Very difficult to put your finger on it. The depopulation of some parts for starters. Young people are leaving and not returning. That is nothing new. It has been going on for decades now. What I find worrying now, particularly, is the pace and the numbers. The Scottish Office seems to be quite happy to invest large sums of money in preserving the wildlife and natural habitat of the Highlands, but very little on the people of the Highlands. The quangos like Scottish Natural Heritage and the special interest groups like RSPB have such enormous political clout that we become fearful for the future of the Highlander. Those bodies seem quite disinterested in the future of the

Highlander just as long as they are in control. Sometimes it comes close to a second Highland clearance. Last time it was in favour of sheep, now it is birds and deer. Everyone talks about preserving the Highlands and the culture, but you can't preserve the past at the expense of the future. They seem to forget that people live and work there too, that people belong there and have done so for centuries. The economies have to grow as well. Maybe I'm not putting that across very well."

"No, I see what you mean."

"Hey, you two come and join the body of the kirk. You are being anti-social," bellowed Charles.

"We'd better join them," said Hector.

The three they joined at the bar now had a rosy glow on their faces and the laughter was becoming more boisterous as time passed.

"Will you have a dram now, Hector?"

"No. I am driving. A juice will be fine."

"Well, a juice it will be. Tom, you are falling behind, man. A large Springbank for you," said Alan.

Tom looked at Hector with raised eyebrows. Hector shrugged his shoulders in sympathy.

"So when are you coming back home, Hecky?" said Alan.

"That isn't up to me."

"Well, I hope it is soon. We miss you. It is time we stopped all that old nonsense. They seem to forget that we are living in a modern age now."

"Yes, and I back up every word he has just said, Hector." said Charles. "Anyway, tell us how you have been faring. Are you being your usual celibate self?"

"Celibate?" said Alan. "Fat chance with what he's got under his kilt. You see," he said by way of explanation to Tom and Lachie, "our wee Hecky has been a naughty boy. Not that that is anything new in the Highlands, it is just that Hector started a bit earlier than most and maybe went at it with more vigour."

"Yes, he went at it like a tinker's dog," said Alan. "You have heard the story about the English lady who asked the Highlander what was worn under his kilt. 'There is nothing worn under my kilt,' he replied. 'It is all in perfect working order.' Well, not only was Hector's in perfect working order, it was working overtime. He discovered what his equipment was really for. What he didn't discover was how to stop. He had wee Bessie Campbell in the family way in no time."

Hector blushed deeply.

"Now stop right there. This conversation is getting out of hand."

"Och, it is all right, Hector. It is just a bit of fun. Have you ever heard from Bessie?"

"Yes, I have. As matter of fact, I am going to meet her tonight. In fact, I'm off just now," he said looking at his watch.

"Och, I'm just so happy for you then."

"Yes, so we are," said Alan. "Give Bessie our love, and all the best to you both. We'll not detain you in that case."

Hector shook hands with Lachie and Tom and the brothers hugged him and slapped his back.

"He's a great boy. We are just so proud of him," said Charles.

Tom noticed their eyes were quite moist.

Chapter Twelve

Well now, let's attend to Tom's education," said Alan. "You can't leave Scotland without learning a little bit about our whisky. You know, Tom, there are not too many of us who are real connoisseurs. Charles here has been drinking whisky for years and still doesn't know a good whisky from a mediocre one."

"My arse," said Charles with vehemence. "This bugger still thinks Islay whiskies are unbeatable. Now they are not bad, but they can't hold a candle to Campbeltown's Springbank."

"Oh God, Lachie, we are about to get the Springbank story again."

"You are. It is a story well worth telling. Your education will never be complete Tom, without hearing about Springbank."

"Bring the bugger a soap box. When he gets on about Springbank, he gets quite lyrical. Well, you'd better get it over with and we'll get on with the serious business of whisky drinking," said Alan.

Charles took hold of the lapels of his kilt jacket and embarked on his oration.

"The Springbank distillery was built about eighteen twenty-eight on the site of one Archibald Mitchell's illicit still. His descendants own and control the distillery to this day. It is one of the most traditional of distilleries: the original buildings are still in use.

"Campbeltowns are traditionally full-flavoured and full-bodied whiskies, famous for their depth of flavour and for their slightly salty tang in the finish. They were referred to as the 'Hector of the West', the deepest voice in the choir. The whisky is best compared to 'sea mist'. Springbank can take long maturation to great advantage. It becomes raisiny and rich."

"Hector, as a name, seems to represent whatever is good and strong in these parts. They even apply it to their best whiskies," thought Tom.

"What a load of shite and he probably got it all from the tourist brochures."

"It is not a load of shite, and I have visited the distillery many, many times, and I haven't finished telling Tom about Springbank."

Alan held his head in his hands.

"As I was saying, every malt distillery is different from every other, but Springbank is more different than any of them and that is because at Springbank the whisky comes first, and that is why Springbank is still revered as a great classic.

"You see Springbank is the only remaining Scotch malt distillery which conducts the entire process itself on a single site it starts with barley, and it ends up with bottled whisky. Springbank's way of making whisky is the traditional way, the labour-intensive way, the way you might have thought had disappeared. The business has remained in the hands of the same family since pre-legal days and they don't keep the stills hammering away, day and night, in pursuit of some productivity record."

"That is a great story, Charles," said Tom. "Thank you very much. You seem to be an expert in the field. I'm surprised you don't make whisky yourself."

"Och, no. That is a field for specialists, and that I am not."

"No, he's a specialist in drinking it. With the amount of Springbank he has put under his belt, he should now be a major shareholder," said Alan.

"It is a fact of life, Tom," said Lachie, "that you will hardly ever get two Highlanders to agree on what is the best malt, but fortunately all malt whiskies are good so they will never be too far out no matter what their preference. It is all down to personal taste in the end. However, I think you have had a good day's sampling of what is on offer and we'll leave it at that for the moment. We don't want you to get staggering drunk. We'll continue with your education a bit later, but for now I think it is time we hit the road. We'd best go look for young Hamish. He will doubtless be chatting up some bird somewhere nearby."

"Och, you are off then," said Charles. "It was great meeting you, Tom, and great renewing our acquaintance with you, Lachie. Enjoy the rest of your stay, Tom, and come back again soon."

"They are a great pair of men, are the Macleans," said Tom as they got on the road south.

"Yes, they have the right idea. Life is not easy for a hill farmer these days. They have to contend with a level of bureaucracy that they are quite frankly not up to and the environmentalists are getting in on the act. The quangos and the special interest groups are taking control and not making life any easier. That is getting to be a sore point with Highlanders. They do not take kindly to being told how to look after their land when in fact they know how to look after things a lot better than anyone else. The Highlander is a natural-born conservationist."

"We get rammed down our throat how much our lifestyle is subsidized, but the money spent on tourism, which they see as the cure-all, means we are stuck with the lower paid wages that go along with tourism. Any industry such as fish-farming, which results in any meaningful employment, is under constant attack. It gets to be a bit like the Indian Reservations were at one time in your country - we can have all the culture we want, but no industry. Unfortunately, there is an increase in many of the attendant social problems like young male suicides and alcoholism. All in all, the Highland way of life is just as endangered as many of the things, which the special interest groups want to preserve. They never stop to think that their takeover of the Highlands and the assaults on our remaining industries amount to economic ethnic cleansing."

"Sorry to be so vehement, but it is just something about which I feel very passionate. You can call it Lachie's lament."

"Oh look, Lachie, Tom. There is something amiss up ahead," said Hamish. "It looks like a car has gone off the road."

"Oh, yes. We'd better stop," said Lachie. "They may need some help."

She was in her room when they returned, propped up on the pillows reading the Tales of Rob Roy MacGregor. They were tales of swashbuckling heroics. She was quite carried away with them. He took her in his arms and kissed her warmly.

"I've missed you."

"And I've missed you, too."

She hugged him to her.

"Do I detect the scent of a brewery?"

"You do not, Madam," he said with feigned indignation. "You do not detect the scent of a brewery. You detect the scent of a distillery."

"Ah, well, something like that; and what is your brand of whisky?"

"I think just about every brand of whisky that exists. Lachie has been seeing to all aspects of my education. He does a thorough job of whatever he tackles, does Lachie."

"Would you like something to eat?"

"No. We had dinner not too long ago. Thanks, but I am just fine. I think I need my bed though."

He undressed just a little unsteadily and climbed into bed and took her in his arms.

"Did you enjoy Braemar?"

"Immensely. I just run out of superlatives very quickly when I even think of Braemar. It is pretty well indescribable."

"You are a day late."

He hesitated.

"Er, eh, yes. With a spot of fishing among other things, the trip took a little longer than we had thought. Am I in the dog box?"

"Of course you are not in the dog box. You will never be in the dog box with me."

She drew him closer to her and he snuggled his head in her breast.

"Thanks, I'm glad of that," he mumbled.

His regular contented breathing told her he had fallen asleep.

.

She continued to hold him in her arms.

"What happened?" she wondered to herself.

She sensed that something was amiss. The story of a fishing trip was not wholly convincing. Did he meet Hector? Was that what was behind it all?

"I can't think that it is. He will tell me some time," she thought. "I must trust him now."

She laid him gently back on the pillows. A contented smile crossed her face. She was mystified, but she trusted him.

The morning sun peeped through the curtains to tell her that there was a new day outside. Charlotte stretched luxuriously.

"Good morning," she called to Tom.

He was sitting in a chair by the window reading the paper as he had his coffee. He poured her a cup and brought it over to her. He placed the cup on her bedside table and took her in his arms and kissed her.

"I wonder if a kiss like that could be considered respectable at this time in the morning," she enquired.

"Who's talking of respectability?"

"Nobody, come to think of it."

"Well in that case, Good Morning."

"This is luxury."

"It is. Let's just enjoy it."

"Tom, I was thinking last night - we have not made any firm travel plans for going back to the States. It is time we thought of going back. The boys' time at the camp is almost up."

"Yes. Maybe we'd better. Let me have a look at the travel section."

"Know what, Honey? The Q.E.2 sails from Southampton tomorrow," said Tom from behind his paper. "Let's see if we can take the Q.E.2 to New York and we can go direct to Vermont and pick up the kids from camp," he said. "We can just about fit all of that in. What do you think?"

"Sounds romantic. I think that would be just great. All kinds of surprises are coming my way these days. I wonder what happened to my staid and respectable old husband?"

"Oh, that old jerk has gone for good. Just forget him, Honey."
Tom ran his hand over her belly.

"Honey, just stick with me. I'll show you all kinds of excitement and good times."

"I'm open to all kinds of offers." She smiled and nibbled his ear.

"So, you will go along with the Q.E.2?"

"I'll go along with it."

"In that case let's call the travel agent."

A warm and comfortable feeling spread through her and she lay back and marveled at her good fortune while he talked on the telephone. It wasn't just herself. It was Tom's life too. His life had changed even more. She was glad now that she had told Tom of her time with Hector. She knew that from now on she and Tom would never be anything less than completely open with each other. She could now be just as adventurous about sex as he was, and without question she found it a very rewarding experience. When she looked at herself in the mirror, she still had difficulty in recognising this soft natural-looking woman who stared back at her. Where had the other sophisticated, hard and brittle woman gone? Charlotte shrugged her shoulders.

"Who cares," she thought.

Tom was still talking on the phone, but he signaled her with thumbs up.

They were reluctant and sorry to leave Morag and Lachie. Charlotte and Morag hugged each other.

"You'll come back soon, won't you?" said Morag, wiping her eyes with the back of her hand.

"Real soon. I promise," said Charlotte with an audible sniff.

Lachie and Morag waved till the car was out of sight.

They had been fortunate to get a good cabin on the promenade deck. She was on her way to meet Tom. As she passed the beauty salon, Charlotte experienced a moment of panic. Inside was a scene she knew very well. The very smell of the hairdryers and the scent of cosmetics were something very familiar to her. She saw, for a fleeting moment, herself as she used to be.

"Six weeks ago I would have been sitting in there eaten up with anxiety about how I looked instead of enjoying myself out on the deck in the sunshine. I feel as if I have been released from a prison sentence," she thought.

Tom was deep in conversation with a plain-looking mature woman when Charlotte joined him.

"Hi, Honey," he said. "Come meet Lady Lomond."

The two women shook hands.

"Lady Lomond is a notable historian. She is on her way to the States to do a lecture tour," said Tom.

"Tom has been telling me of your trip through the Highlands of Scotland. It sounds like you have had a wonderful trip. Ah! What a history they have, the Scots. It is violent and bloody and heroic and romantic, all at the same time."

"Yes, I found the country quite bewitching in so many ways," said Charlotte. "How interesting that you are a historian. I have never before met a historian. You know, Tom too has resurrected a long-buried love of history. I never even knew it existed."

"Do you mind that?"

"No, not at all."

"Well, I have to warn you that it can become very absorbing. Once you get into it, it can take over your life."

"I don't think I shall mind too much."

"Then that is to the good. It will fit in with your ranch life, too."

"Oh! Are we to have a ranch life?" Charlotte smiled.

"I just mentioned it as a possibility. We have not yet made up our minds," said Tom.

"I think you have already made up your minds. You just don't yet relise that fact," said Lady Lomond. "I shall be very surprised if, one year from now, you Tom are not both a rancher and a historian."

Chapter Thirteen

They leaned over the rail and looked out over the ocean. The moon laid a Silvery path over the water. The night was now quiet. They could hear the swish of the water as the bows cut through the gentle swell. Tom's arm went round her shoulder.

"Time for bed."

"Oh, Tom, just a little longer. This is our last night. It is so beautiful. It is so peaceful."

"Yes, isn't it? Strange how it took us so long to find out just how good life can be. How much have we missed?"

"We mustn't think of that, Tom. I think we must just be thankful that we did find out and just make sure that we never fall into the rat race trap again. Just think how many people never find that out."

When they got to the cabin, Tom poured drinks for both of them.

"I have to tell you something, Honey. I don't know if this is the right time. I don't know if there is ever a right time for such things, but I have to tell you. It is the reason why we were late coming back from Braemar."

"I thought there was something. I have had the feeling ever since the night you returned. Tom, remember what we agreed that day. We must never keep anything from each other."

"I know, Honey, but this is rough, very rough. For days I've been looking for a way to tell you gently. There isn't a way."

"Then tell me. Tell me anyway. It concerns Hector, doesn't it?"

"Yes. Lachie introduced me to Hector."

"Was there..? I mean, did you … did you quarrel with him?"

"No, put your mind at rest on that score. You see, Charlotte, I am increasingly conscious of just what I owe to that young man. I know now that you and our boys mean everything in life to me. I also know that I came perilously close to losing my family life. We had drifted much further far apart than either of us realised. I think you knew that too. That is why you took the trip in the first place. That was woman's instinct. You were very fortunate to meet someone who could help you along the road. Everything that is now good in our lives starts from there."

"You are a good man, Tom."

"I don't know so much. There are quite a few things I have done that I am not very proud of. You have to do such things to survive in that world these days, but I am still not very proud of a lot of them. This last four weeks has opened my eyes. I can't ever go back to that lifestyle now."

"You are a good man, but tell me what happened."

"Yes. We first met two of his brothers in a pub called The Brig. That whole day had a surreal feel about it. The magnificent scenery belongs in postcards and calendars. The colour and spectacle and pageantry of the games could be from any epic film and to top it all there was the Royal Family."

"It was something which I wouldn't have missed for the world. I felt greatly privileged just to be there. I was still on a high when we went to The Brig and there were those two larger than life men. They greeted Lachie like a long-lost brother. Lachie just introduced me as his friend Tom from the States. Hector joined his brothers shortly after. They are all of a mould are the Maclean men, but what a magnificent mould. The two brothers are older and they are big boisterous men who love life and whisky. Hector is just as you described him. He is more striking with his auburn hair and those hazel eyes. He came in for a lot of teasing from his brothers, but also a lot of affection and congratulation. They are obviously a close- knit family, the Macleans. Hector had turned in a magnificent performance at the Games. He was the youngest competitor there by quite a long way, but he had more than his share of silverware. He also had the open admiration of such aficionados as Lachie and that is not lightly bestowed.

"We got a chance to talk together, on our own, for a while. At one point we found ourselves on one side. He is a highly intelligent young man. Our conversation was coloured by what I knew of him. I had great difficulty keeping myself from divulging that knowledge. He told me he had to leave then to go to meet someone. His brothers were teasing him. They were a bit naughty in the down to earth way of people who work so close to nature. They told us about the girlfriend whom he had put in the family way and that he hadn't seen her for more than two years. It was then that he told them that he and Bessie had arranged to meet in Perth after the games. Of course I knew of Bessie and the son they had. I felt so happy for him then and so did his brothers.

"We spent quite some more time with the brothers, Charles and Alan. They insisted in educating me in the art of choosing and drinking malt. Of course they could never agree on which was the best malt whisky, although they seem to have got through them all at one time or another. It was Lachie who insisted that we find Hamish and get on the road south."

"You seem to have had a great time and I am so glad for you that you took the chance."

"We had a great time. The best you could imagine. We had another drink with Charles and Allan, and then we said goodbye to them. We were the first to come across Hector. He was sitting with his back to a rock. He held her in his arms and blood and tears were streaming down his face.

"She'll be all right in just a wee while," he said.

"She lay just like a rag doll. We knew then that she was far from all right. I stayed with Hector while Lachie went to get help. Hector traveled in the ambulance with her. We followed him in our car and we waited with him while they took her into emergency. I managed to persuade him to have a wash. I think he knew then that there was little hope. I called his Aunt in Glasgow for him and I told her what had happened. She must have left right then. She arrived at the hospital three hours later. She was a plump, capable and caring woman and it was obvious that she adored Hector. She was what he needed just then. Lachie had also succeeded in getting hold of Charles and Alan. We all stayed the night in Perth. We went to see him before we left in the morning. Charles and Alan took us to the side to tell us that the prognosis was not good. It was very likely that she would be paralysed for the rest of her life. Hector sat by her bed and held her hand all the time. She looked so well lying back on the pillows and smiling up at him as he stroked her nut-brown hair. I have never felt so desperately sorry for anyone as I did for that young couple then."

Silent tears now ran unchecked down Charlotte's cheeks and he put his arms round her and pulled her closer to him.

"It is best that I tell you all of it."

She nodded her head.

"There was not a lot more that we could do for him. It was a time for family. He had his Aunt and Charles and Alan and so we bade him goodbye. He saw us off. He embraced us both on the hospital steps. He was so full of gratitude. I felt guilty then. What I had done for him was nothing compared with what he had done for us, but there was no way I could ever tell him that. I vowed then that if ever the opportunity arose where I could do anything for him, then I would certainly do so. That is a vow I intend to keep if I ever get the chance.

"We pieced the details together later from what he told us and what the police could discover. She couldn't wait for him to come to Perth.. She drove along the road to meet him and her car went out of control just outside of Perth. Her steering had broken. It was Hector who found her car upended in the ditch. She would have died there and then if it hadn't been for him. It required superhuman strength to get the car out of the ditch. No one could ever work out how he managed it, but he did. He practically tore the car to pieces with his bare hands to get her out. Charles and Allan stayed on in Perth to be with him. Lachie phoned them a couple of times to find out how they had fared. Hector sat by her bedside for two days. She was conscious and had no pain. At least they had great happiness for that time, but then she suffered a brain hemorrhage and died."

Tom held Charlotte ever closer in his arms and stroked her as she sobbed. He too was crying and together they grieved for the sadness of their friend.

Hector

It had been a long time. The farmyard looked much the same as it had always done. He stood by the barn door and surveyed the scene, which were his childhood and his home. A sturdy little boy emerged from the dairy and walked over to him. Hector picked him up. The shock of hair was black as the raven's wing and the eyes blue as the sea, but the features were those he saw every morning in the mirror. There was tightness in his chest and tears welled in his eyes as he hugged his son to him.

"Yes, she said I was to take care of you and I shall. I have something to live for. I have you to live for and I could not wish for better. Live for you I shall. I promise you that."

He kissed his son and hugged him close again before he put him down. Hand in hand they walked towards the house.

Chapter Fourteen

They looked out over a vista of yellow and gold, orange and crimson and dark green blue. Soon the trees would be stark and bare and the winter snows would come but for the moment the forest was dressed in all her glory. Nowhere is the fall more spectacular than in Vermont. Charlotte, Tom and the boys had found a quiet pine lodge high on the hillside in which to have their lunch.

"So how was camp? Asked Tom when they were seated.

"Oh yeah, the camp was all right," they said.

There was little enthusiasm in their voices.

"You don't sound too impressed."

"Oh, it was okay, I guess," said Mike. "But it is too crowded. There are just too many guys there."

"So maybe now you need a bit of space and a bit of quiet."

"It would help."

"Well, how does a trip through the States grab you?" asked Tom.

A look approaching distrust crossed their faces.

"Oh yeah! Sounds great," said Gary, "but who all will be going on the trip?"

"Why, all of us," Tom replied.

"Can you spare the time? I mean."

"I can see that there are all kinds of questions coming into your minds," said Tom. "Will you keep them just for the moment and trust us. There will be answers, but they will take time. We have a lot of explaining to do, we have a lot to talk about, and we have a lot of planning to do. We'll take it slowly."

It had been one of those mornings, which required tact and understanding.

"Do I look very different Tom?" asked Charlotte, as they drove up the mountain towards the camp. She was just a little concerned about how the new image would be received. Tom took a sideways glance at her. She wore a soft fawn jersey wool dress with a lamb's wool cardigan over it and plain shoes. Gone was the over-emphasized jewelry, which she used to wear. Now she wore a simple gold chain with a small Celtic cross. Her hair was soft and natural and if she wore makeup it was not noticeable. There was an air of calm

91

confidence about her. Tom thought she had never looked more beautiful. He too was casual in wool slacks and a roll neck lambs wool sweater.

"You look just great, Babe."

"Do you think they will approve?"

"They couldn't do anything but. Relax, Honey, everything is going to work out just fine."

"Oh, Tom, I hope so. We have changed, you know, both of us. What do you think their reaction is going to be?"

"Cultural shock at the very least."

The boys were waiting on the porch. They were surprised to see both their parents together. That was something they had seen very little of in the past few years. Charlotte could see the bewilderment in their faces as she and Tom stepped from the car. She walked up to them and in turn threw her arms round them in a bear hug, which left them open-mouthed. This was not the gentle peck on the cheek they had become accustomed to. Tom's greeting was no less heart-warming.

"So what you are suggesting is a trip through the States for all of us?"

"Yes. That is if you would like to."

"Oh, yes please," they all replied at once.

They drove straight to the airport.

"Now, if we are going to travel like bums we can't take all of this baggage," said Tom.

They sorted out the heavy baggage and Tom and Mike carried it over to the freight desk and shipped it off direct to Beaumont. They each kept only one light hold all of casual clothes. They bought a map and studied it over a cup of coffee.

"Let's be realistic. We can't cover all of the States," said Tom. "Has anyone any preferences?"

"We've seen enough of the Northern States," said Gary. "Why can't we start somewhere in the middle."

"I agree," said Charlotte.

They flew to Raleigh, North Carolina, and then west to Greensboro in West Virginia. It was the quietest of rural settings. They rented a car at the airport and drove out till they came to a little motel. Dusk was falling in the sleepy little hamlet. There were only two other cars parked in the yard and wood smoke rose lazily from the stone chimney. Their welcome was warm and the rooms were clean and comfortable. The food was home-cooked, simple and quite delicious. Charlotte tucked into the thick juicy steak with French fries and salad and then into the apple pie and ice cream. Bob's eyebrows rose.

"You don't think you might put on a pound or two," remarked Bob.

"I might just do that and what is more I don't care."

"It won't go down to well in Beaumont," said Gary,

"That's just too bad."

"The guys at high school all have mothers who are slim and made up and their hair all done up every day."

"Yes, and they all have sour expressions to match just like I used to have," said Charlotte. "Of course, if you want I could always go back to that."

"Don't dare think of it or we shall disown you," said Mike.

They sat round the log fire replete and content after their meal.

"I think it is time we had a talk," said Tom. "You have all been very patient and thanks for trusting your mother and me. Now that we are all fed I think we can talk. I know I said we could catch up with all of this later and we shall, but maybe I had better explain a bit right now. I'll put things as concisely as I can just now and we'll put the flesh on the bones as we travel."

"Your mother got the feeling there had to be more to life than Beaumont was offering. She and Connie took themselves off to Europe. They started off in Scotland and that was as far as your mother got. She took time out to think and Scotland is a great place to think. She liked the experience. She called me one night when I was in the middle of the biggest deal of my life. She asked me to sell out everything and come and join her. She gave me all of the right reasons and I just sold out there and then. I joined her in Scotland and we stayed there for over four weeks. We wandered like a pair of bums and then we came back on the Q.E.2."

"We kind of like what we have discovered. We don't want to go back to the old Beaumont lifestyle. Maybe we don't want to go back to Beaumont. We can consider alternatives. We didn't want to make too many plans till we had a chance to talk things over with you. We are thinking in terms of a lifestyle that is less tied up in the rat race, something maybe a little closer to nature. What I would like you to do is give some thought to what you would like for the future. We may not go along with what you decide, but I promise you we shall listen. We shall take plenty time to listen, but maybe you had better be thinking in terms of working summers instead of expensive summer camps all the time."

"I don't want to sound ungrateful," said Mike, "but if I never saw another summer camp, I shouldn't miss it. I don't think I would be sorry to see the back of Beaumont either. I think I speak for the others too."

"Too right you do," they said.

"Fine! Now let's sit back and plan the journey. I reckon we can spare ten days to get to Beaumont. We'll need all of that time. How does that go down with you all?"

"Sounds just great," said Mike.

In the quiet of their bedroom, she and Tom mused on the day and on their sons.

"They are full of fun and mischief, Tom. We have never had fun like this with our kids."

"No, we've never taken the time, but let's just enjoy them."

"Shall we tell them we are thinking of a ranch?"

"Not yet. Let's hold off for a week or so. I think we had better give them the chance to come up with their own ideas first."

"Yes, I think you are right. Oh, Tom I am so happy."

"Yes, me too."

They wandered slowly west till they reached the Mississippi. They sat on the edge of a levee and watched the magnificent Mississippi paddle steamers wend their way majestically along the calm lazy river.

"Gee, it would be great to go for a bit by steamboat," said Bob dreamily.

"Well, why not?" said Charlotte.

"I think Louisiana is getting to them," said Tom. "I think we'd better find a steam boat."

They took a steamboat for a long way downstream. Their ten days were drawing quickly to a close.

"Oh, gee, we want to see something of the other end of Texas," said the boys.

"We'll have to make it a quick trip then," said Tom.

They stopped at a little motel in a small town somewhere near Amarillo in the heart of the Texas Panhandle. A notice on the edge of the town welcomed them to San Miguel and told them there was to be a rodeo next day.

"Oh, please, let's see it," the boys pleaded.

"Well, it will have to be our last fling. We shall have to head direct for Beaumont right after this."

"Okay," they agreed.

Their interest in the countryside had surprised Charlotte and Tom. It was an interest, which grew as they traveled.

Chapter Fifteen

Charlotte was sick next morning and Tom was full of concern.

"It's nothing serious," she reassured him. "Something I ate or a bug I picked up."

"Let's find a doctor then."

"Oh, it will pass."

Tom was insistent and she went along with him.

"Don't let me spoil your day then. You and the boys can have a look round town while I am at the doctor and I shall meet you back here for coffee at mid-morning."

Tom and the boys were in great high spirits when they rejoined her. This was ranching country and the town was full of cowboys in town for the rodeo. Tom and the boys were all wearing Stetsons. Charlotte looked up and smiled.

"If those guys had had their way, they would have bought horses as well," said Tom.

The rodeo was a thrill for all of them. They ate popcorn and munched on hot dogs and drank root beer as they watched men on the bucking broncos and marveled at the tenacity as the lean hard muscular men clung to the wildly cavorting bulls beneath them. Charlotte was soon caught up with the enthusiasm that surrounded her. She was no mean horsewoman herself, but her experience had been limited to the more seemly events of New England. This was more raw and thrilling stuff. It captivated her. She avidly read what she could glean from the brochures she had picked up.

The origins of the rodeo may be traced to the early days of the American cattle industry in the mid-nineteenth century, she read. Once or twice each year, cowhands rounded up cattle on the ranges and drove the herds to various marketing centers. There, in celebration of the roundups, they staged informal competitions to exhibit the skills of their trade. The first formal rodeo contest probably was held in Cheyenne in 1872, but this is not known for certain.

A rodeo is essentially a competitive sport in which riders display their skill in activities related directly or indirectly to livestock raising, such as riding and roping cattle and horses. The term rodeo comes from the Spanish word rodear (to surround) and originally meant 'roundup'. A rodeo usually comprises five standard events and may also include up to three non-standard events, as well as a number of informal contests. The main events are saddle bronco riding, bareback bronco riding, bull riding, steer wrestling, and calf roping. (A bronco is a horse that bucks, or, when mounted, tries to throw off a rider.) Barrel racing can also be included, usually as a sport for female riders only. Team roping and steer roping are also popular.

Charlotte nudged Tom to draw his attention to the boys. They sat on the edge of their seats, with their mouths open and totally absorbed and captivated by the scene in front of them. Their knuckles were white as they gripped the edges of their seats. Each in his imagination was sitting astride the cavorting broncos.

"I don't think we shall have to work too hard at selling the idea of a ranch to them," she whispered.

The boys met up with young men of their own age and disappeared halfway through the afternoon. The rodeo was almost finished when Tom and Charlotte went to look for them. They found them some way from the rodeo ground, all on horseback and being schooled in the art of roping steers by their newfound friends. From the expressions on their faces Charlotte could see they were enthralled with the experience.

"You won't mind if we stay here for a spell?" Mike asked. "We want to go into town with the guys. We can meet you back at the motel."

"I don't know," said Charlotte. "This is a strange place. It appears all right, but we don't know too much about it. We don't want you to come to harm."

"Gee, Mom, I'm seventeen now and this is ranching country. Bad things don't happen here. Just for a little while, Mom ... one of the guys will drop us back."

"Oh, all right - but be careful."

"We have to let go of them some time," she said to Tom as they sped off with their new friends.

"Are you all right? You seem quiet and thoughtful," said Tom.

"Yes, I'm fine, just fine. Well, at least ..."

Charlotte took hold of Tom's hand and held it.

"Tom, I am glad we have this moment to ourselves. There is something I want to tell you." She hesitated. "I ... I'm pretty sure I'm pregnant. I am going to have a baby."

He took her in his arms and kissed her for a long time.

"That is wonderful news. It delights me," he said at last.

"But, Tom, have you thought this through? There could be complications. There was Hector, too, you know."

"Yes, of course there was Hector too. Do you have any opinions, any indications?"

"No, Tom. I have been looking at it from every angle. Tom, I have just no way of telling. That is the truth."

"Then don't let it concern you."

"But, Tom, I may be having another man's child!"

"It will be your child too."

"Yes, but Tom, I mean ... what I want to say is abhorrent to me, but if you really want me to, I can't even put it into words, but you know what I mean. I ... I'll do it."

"You'd do that for me?"

She nodded.

"Even though you find it abhorrent?"

"Yes, Tom."

"Then, I am greatly honored. More honored than I have ever been in my life. I also feel very humble right now."

He sat quiet for just a moment.

"But, Honey, don't ever think what you can't even put into words. The thought is equally abhorrent to me. It isn't just my Irish antecedents - I could never think of destroying a life. I could never live with myself. And you couldn't either if you are honest."

"No, Tom. I couldn't."

"Then let's forget it. Why are we talking like this, anyway, in the face of the best thing that's happened to us in years? What better way to start a new chapter than with a new life? I'm just thrilled."

"But Tom, you are not facing the reality, the possibilities."

"Oh, yes, I am. I'm facing them full and square. Look, Charlotte, you're going to have a child. It will be your child. It may be our child. Let's wait and see. If I am not the father, we shall have to take a decision as to whether we let Hector know. Either way I shall love it unreservedly. In fact I love her, him to bits already."

"Why do you say 'her' first?"

"I don't know, a hunch maybe. I'm not too bothered what sex it is. I just think a wee girl would be specially nice."

"Tom, I'm so relieved, just so relieved."

"Then let's put all that behind us now. It does explain the appetite though."

"Hmm, yes, doesn't it? Shall we tell the boys?"

"I suggest we hold off a little bit. They have had so much that is new on their plate of late. Let's wait till we get back to Beaumont."

"Oh, Tom, I'm worried about them," said Charlotte. "Don't you think we should go look for them?"

"No, Charlotte, I don't. There are times when we have to trust them and show our trust too. I think this is one of those times. Let's give them another half-hour."

Charlotte agreed, but she sat twisting her handkerchief. Tom had gone to the bar to get them a drink when she was called to the telephone. Her heart pounded as she lifted the phone.

"Mrs. Benson?" inquired the voice in a Texas drawl. "I'm Mary Alice Ferguson and we ranch a little piece out of San Miguel and I just called to tell you that we have your boys right here."

"Are they all right?" gasped Charlotte.

"Sure. They are right as rain. No need to worry about those boys. They are having the time of their lives, and, if I may say so, that is a great bunch of boys you have. They came out with my boys, Sam and Charlie, and we are real happy to have them here. I'm sorry, I didn't realise till just now that you didn't know where they were and I thought you might be worrying."

"I was. I was very worried and I am greatly relieved to know they are all right and thank you very much for calling to tell me. I feel much better now."

Charlotte instinctively liked the voice at the other end of the telephone. The tone was calm and dependable.

"Then I'm glad," said Mary Alice. "You don't mind if they stay and have a bite of supper with us? I'll send them right back as soon as they are finished and I hope you will allow them to come back out tomorrow."

"You are very kind to ask them. Are you sure it isn't too much trouble?"

"No trouble at all."

"Then they can certainly stay for supper and thank you very much, but I'm afraid it won't be possible for them to come tomorrow. You see we have to leave early to get back to Beaumont by nightfall. The boys start school the day after."

"I am real sorry to hear that. I hope you will allow them to come back one day soon."

The boys tumbled from the pickup as it screeched to a halt. They got out in a tangle of Stetsons and cowboy boots and blue jeans and check shirts. There seemed to be an army of young men, but there were only seven of them. Mike introduced their friends.

"This is Charlie and Sam Ferguson and James and Andrew McIvor."

The boys removed their Stetsons and shook hands all round. They were polite and courteous young men.

"Gee, Ma'am," said Charlie, the eldest of the lot, "I am real sorry we kept Mike and Bob and Gary out for so long and I do hope I have not given you any cause for concern."

"Not at all Charlie. We feel the boys are old enough now to take care of themselves," said Charlotte, belying her concern of an hour ago.

Mike threw her a look, which spoke sheer gratitude. His chest puffed with pride.

"Then I hope, Ma'am, that you will allow them to come back out to the ranch tomorrow."

"That's kind of you, Charlie, but it won't be possible," said Tom. "You see, we have to reach Beaumont by tomorrow night and that means an early start but thanks again for asking them."

There was a crestfallen silence. For some time no one spoke. The disappointment was almost tangible. It was Sam who broke the silence.

"Well, Sir, you do have to eat before you go and our ranch is just a little way out of town on the highway south. Couldn't you at least come for breakfast?"

"Oh, we couldn't trouble your folks to that extent," said Charlotte.

"Oh, no trouble at all, I assure you. We shall be real pleased to have you all," said Charlie.

"Please, please, please, Mom," Bob pleaded.

Charlotte looked at Tom. He nodded assent.

"Well, if you are sure it won't put your folks out any."

"None at all, Ma'am. I assure you."

Charlotte was putting the finishing touches to her packing when Tom came in.

"There's a plot hatching out there. The air is heavy with conspiracy," he smiled.

"What makes you say that?"

"Well, the boys are in a huddle and they are either talking in whispers or yelling at each other. The moment I appear they clam up."

"So, what's it all about?"

"I have no idea, but I think we are going to find out quite soon."

The Fergusons were a pleasant solid dependable couple who had been ranching there for most of their lives. The ranch house was a big sprawling comfortable place. Charlotte fell in love with the Fergusons and their house right away. Tom too was very impressed. They had breakfast on the porch. The morning was fresh and bright and clean and they could see for miles. It was little wonder that the Fergusons were so happy with their lot. Ben Ferguson kept fondly looking at the boys.

"Thank you so much for having us, Ben. I'll remember this for a long time. So will the boys."

"They'd make a good bunch of ranchers would those boys you have there."

"They have never been on a ranch in their lives."

"I have," said Ben.

Tom looked at his watch. The boys had excused themselves to go have a look at a young colt.

"Relax Tom," said Ben. "What's another day? It won't be the end of the world if you don't make Beaumont tonight or tomorrow night for that matter."

"The boys do have to go back to school tomorrow," said Charlotte, but there was no great conviction in her voice.

"It wouidn't be the end of the world if they miss a day or two."

"No you're right, but I don't want to impose on your hospitality."

"Never give it a thought. We enjoy your company." He sat back and lit his pipe.

He talked about ranching. He loved the life and his love of ranching was infectious. It somehow seeped into their being. Charlotte looked at Tom and his eyes were bright with interest. She felt a thrill the likes of which she had not felt in a long time. She knew then that this must be their life from now on. She knew that they would have to start looking for a ranch soon. She knew it must be very soon.

"I can't understand how folks could give up a life like this to go live in a city," went on Ben, "but that is just what I think my neighbors over on Bar C are about to do. She is hankering after a city life and he can't seem to make up his mind. If someone was to make him an offer tomorrow he would be off to the city right away."

"Life is strange," said Charlotte. "We have a house in Beaumont and if some one would make us an offer we would high tail it out of there tomorrow too."

"Then why don't you have a look at the Bar C? You could do a nice trade there."

"Hey, steady on, Ben," said Tom. "I admit we have been thinking of a ranch, but we have to think about it a lot more. We would have to talk to the boys."

"No problem there. They love the Bar C."

"They've never seen the Bar C."

"Oh yes they have. They had a good look over it yesterday. Our boys took them there after the rodeo. They talked of nothing else all during supper."

"So that is what the plotting was all about. Well, I'll be damned."

Tom shook his head and smiled

"Then why not give it a look over? You needn't feel obligated. There is no reason why you shouldn't have a look, at least," said Ben.

"There's Beaumont."

"Beaumont is a long way away."

Chapter Sixteen

A horse came into sight up the dusty road. It was being ridden at a gallop.

"It's Liz. That's our daughter," said Mary Alice.

Liz went over to join the boys. She was a slim beautiful sixteen-year-old. Charlotte could see the interest in Mike's eyes

"I think we should go look at a ranch, Tom," she said.

"I think we had better ask about the business side first."

Ben had been a successful rancher for years. He was well qualified to advise Tom and Charlotte. For over an hour they discussed land values and stock values and the costs involved and the returns they could expect. His predictions were far better than Tom could have hoped for.

"I think there could be a dollar or two in ranching," he said to Charlotte.

"Then you will have a look at the Bar C."

"I think we must. Beaumont will have to wait for one more day."

"Fine! You and I will ride over to the Bar C. Mary Alice can take Charlotte over in the truck."

Charlotte was very impressed with her husband as he easily and confidently mounted the quarter horse, which Charlie had saddled up for him. She was even more impressed as her sons appeared round the corner of the barn. They sat on their horses as though they had been born in the saddle. They followed Ben and Tom over to the Bar C. Ben pointed out all the things they should be looking for as he and Tom rode over to the ranch.

"Oh, Mary Alice, can we stop just here?"

"Of course we can. You want to see the view. It is well worth a good look."

Charlotte was enraptured. Ahead of them at the top of a small hillock was one of the most attractive old ranch houses she had ever seen. It was in the Old Spanish style with deep verandahs and graceful archways almost all the way round and it was festooned with creepers of all kinds. It was a weathered and comfortable old house and Charlotte fell quite in love with it even from this distance.

"Do you like it?" said Mary Alice.

"It is quite quite beautiful," said Charlotte in a hushed voice.

"You'll like it even better close up."

Louis Mahler and his wife Sarah gave them a warm welcome. Mary Alice was right - Charlotte did like the house even more the closer they got to it. It was built round a patio, which was shaded by a splendid old spreading fig tree. The flagstones shone like polished mahogany and comfortable chairs were carelessly spread out in the shade. Sarah brought them coffee on a silver tray. Charlotte wandered over to the edge of the verandah. She had a few moments quite to herself. The rolling country captivated her. Away in the distance she could see a solitary pine tree atop a ridge. It looked lonely and majestic.

"I will go there one day soon," she thought, and then she took a grip on herself.

"Steady on," she reminded herself. "We are just looking the place over."

But deep within herself she was silently praying.

"It is beautiful, isn't it?" Louis Mahler's voice interrupted her reverie.

"Very beautiful indeed."

"I think you will buy it."

"What!" She was taken aback.

"You will buy it."

"We are just looking. A decision on buying is still some way off."

"I know that, but you will."

"Anything in particular which makes you think that?"

He smiled a warm smile. He took her arm and led her to the verandah round the side of the house.

"Look over there towards that clump of trees."

Charlotte spied a group of men on horseback. They were still too far off to recognise, but she guessed it must be Ben and Tom and the boys.

"They look like a sheriff's posse," she smiled.

"Your husband apart, they have all been here before."

"Oh, yes. I must apologise. I do hope they didn't cause you any inconvenience."

"None at all. Think nothing of it. It was a pleasure to have them. I have to warn you, though. They are very keen on this ranch. They are very polite young men, are your sons. You have good reason to be proud of them."

"And I am."

"The middle one, Gary, did offer a trade - your house in Beaumont in exchange for the ranch."

She smiled and put her hand on his arm.

"I do apologise."

"Think nothing of it. It might be an idea, though. Is that something you might consider?"

Charlotte smiled.

"I'm sorry. I should not have put the idea to you like that, but would you give it some thought and I think you should have a look round the house before they get here."

"Perhaps I had better."

Sarah Mahler took Charlotte round the house. She was slender and dark-haired and her beauty was in the classic tradition. Charlotte noticed her hands first. They were slender and beautiful hands. They were the hands of an artiste. The house was cool and elegantly furnished in the Mexican tradition. Sarah had impeccable taste. The furniture and décor were in quiet harmony with the house and the landscape.

"You have perfect taste," said Charlotte. "This is a marvelous effect which you have achieved."

"Yes, I am quite proud of it."

"But you want to leave it." She sighed deeply.

"Oh, it is so difficult to decide."

"I'm sorry. That was tactless of me."

"No. Look! You seem a woman who is happy with herself. You don't mind my saying that."

"Not at all.

"Will you sit down? I would like to ask you something, if I may. Please."

"Certainly."

They were in the large cool master bedroom. There was an elegant tapestry chaise longue by the window. They sat down facing each other. Sarah seemed tense and Charlotte took hold of one long slim hand and held it. Slowly Sarah began to relax.

"When I saw you step down from the pickup you looked as though you were at peace with the world and you looked so self-assured. I thought I could talk with this woman. Can I?"

"Of course you can."

"It is difficult."

"I know. Just tell me what you tell yourself in moments of quiet."

"Ah, yes. What I tell myself."

"Three years ago I lost my child. It was stillborn and I cannot have any more children. For me my world ended. I had given up my dream to have a child. I was happy to do so, but in the end I had neither. I could not stay in Dallas and Louis brought me here. He too gave up his dream. We found some peace here. Ben and Mary Alice have been good kind friends and there has been some measure of contentment. It was all right up till a few months ago and then my dream returned to haunt me. I am a pianist. I think I can be a good pianist if I try, but something holds me back."

Charlotte remained silent. This was an unexpected role for her. It was not unwelcome. She felt complimented that some one should confide in her and seek her advice.

"You see," Sarah continued, "Louis also gave up his dream to take me here. He is so good, my Louis. He never complains, but I think in his heart he longs for the world of commerce and business deals. We could be fairly content here. We like ranching quite well. Maybe we could come to love it if we give ourselves the chance. We did think of selling up and we told Mary Alice and Ben, and then we had second thoughts. That is how it has been for us. I had almost decided that is what we should do and then a bunch of young men came calling. One of them suggested we do a trade."

"Why not Beaumont? I thought. It has a good conservatoire and Louis would be happy in the world of oil deals. We talked late into the night. Oh, I don't know. Is it wrong to follow your dream? Is it self-indulgence? Is it weakness? Perhaps it is and then we may not find our dreams. We might end up with illusions instead."

"There is one thing I can tell you now," said Charlotte. "It is not weakness nor self-indulgence to follow your dream. Following your dream requires courage, sometimes great courage. Following your dream requires faith. It is not always easy. It is never dull. Sometimes it can be exciting. It is always worthwhile. I should know. That is what Tom and I are doing right now. Sarah, follow your dream. You must. There is no other way. Let me tell you a story."

"Does it have a happy ending? I could not bear to hear it otherwise."

"I don't know if it has a happy ending. We haven't got there yet, but I have faith. I think you should hear it."

Charlotte recounted her experiences of the past two months. She left out her meeting with Hector. That was between her and Tom only, but she told Sarah all the rest of what had happened to them. When she had finished she looked up at Sarah. There was a strange expression in her eyes. It was as though she was looking far into the future and without fear.

"Yes, yes," she said. "What a beautiful story. Yes, it has to be like that."

For a moment she seemed to be in another world.

"Do you know Bibi Morgenstern in Beaumont?" she asked.

"Yes, I know Bibi. We serve on many committees together. I know her very well."

"She is my aunt. I called her last night. Somehow the person she described is not like you."

"No, Bibi would not recognise me now. My own sons hardly recognised me. I hardly recognise myself at times."

"And this is your dream?"

"I think so."

"Bibi tells me you have a beautiful house there."

"Yes. It is beautiful, but I prefer this one."

"Then shall we exchange houses and follow our dreams?"

"I think we may have a deal."

Charlotte ran down the road to meet Tom. He dismounted and took her hand in his while he led the horse with his other hand.

"We'll see you up at the Ranch House, Tom," called Ben. He was sensitive. He knew they needed time alone together.

"Do you like it?"

"I love it, and you."

"I haven't seen the inside of the house yet, but if it looks anything like the outside I shall love it too. The rest of the ranch looks pretty good."

"Oh, Tom, it is beautiful inside. It is a kindly, friendly house. I felt that the moment I went into it."

"That is the best possible starting place."

"Oh, Tom let's sit under this tree while I tell you about Sarah."

Charlotte took her time in telling the sad enchanting story of Sarah. She was solemn as she told Tom of the heartache and the courage and the dreams.

"Oh, Tom," she said, "Shall we exchange dreams? Tom, I feel I could do that if you and the boys like the ranch."

"I somehow think we shall not have much trouble in persuading the boys. In fact, I think if we decided against, they would stay here anyway."

Sarah was serving coffee on the patio. The faces of the boys were expectant and just a bit apprehensive. They were sitting on the edge of their chairs. Charlotte and Tom spent quite some time going round the house with Louis. After some time Sarah came to join them.

"If you don't come to a decision quite soon, those young men on the patio will have chewed themselves up completely," she smiled

"Then we had better go put them at their ease," said Tom.

Things happened very quickly after that. Louis called Sarah's uncle in Beaumont and he went and looked over Tom and Charlotte's house. It was a prime property and he soon came up with a valuation, which was agreeable to Tom and Charlotte and they struck a bargain there and then.

They returned to Ben's ranch for lunch.

"This calls for a celebration," said Ben, as he brought out a bottle of Bourbon. "It isn't every day we get such a fine bunch of new young neighbours."

Charlotte smiled over the rim of her glass.

"Ben Ferguson, I think you engineered a lot of what went on today."

"Not guilty, Ma'am. Let's just say I didn't discourage what I knew to be right, and it will be right. Just you wait and see."

Charlotte kissed him on the cheek.

"Whatever way, I shall always be grateful to you and Mary Alice, but I suppose it will be back to the motel for a few days till we get things sorted out."

"No! Now, that would not be a neighbourly thing to do," said Ben. "You must all stay right here with us till you are ready to move into your ranch."

"But it may take two weeks, Ben," said Tom.

"It may take four weeks or even six. What does that matter? You must stay here with us. Isn't that right, Mary Alice?

"Of course it is right. Huh! Motel indeed."

Over lunch they discussed the future and made plans for the next few days. Charlotte and Tom were to go to Beaumont to finalise the deal and ship the household effects to the ranch. The Mahlers were planning to move in two days.

"We'll take the boys into town and get them enrolled in the high school tomorrow," said Mary Alice. "The school starts next week. Meantime they can get to grips with some cattle ranching."

"I keep getting the idea that all of this might just have been prearranged," said   Charlotte.

"Well, not exactly prearranged," said Mary Alice, " but I do admit that we did talk about it a little last night. You see, those boys had their heart set on that ranch and we kind of thought this might happen and so we just did a little more planning."

"Tom, I think we are being railroaded."

"Well, the train is going in the direction we want to go in, anyway. So who cares?"

The boys stayed with Ben and Mary Alice for two weeks. During that time they started school and learned a great deal about horses and about cattle ranching. They were never short of teachers. Sam and Charley taught them all they knew of the art of roping steers and the more showy aspects of horsemanship. Ben saw that they had a good grounding in the more practical aspects of ranching.

Mike just happened to be in the yard when Liz went out riding next morning.

"Want to come along?" she asked.

"Yeah, I suppose I could," he said nonchalantly.

"I go out quite a way and I go fast. Do you think you are up to it?"

"I'm up to it."

But he wasn't. The outward trot was all right, but his horse stumbled on the gallop homeward and Mike flew out of the saddle and ended up in a clump of prickly pear.

"Are you all right?" called Liz.

He stood up, red, angry and embarrassed, with cactus spines sticking out of his clothing, his hair and his person.

"You look like a porcupine," laughed Liz, and his face grew even redder.

He redoubled his efforts in learning to ride. He did not go out riding again with Liz.

The Bensons took over the ranch complete with all the stock, quarter horses and equipment. That first weekend after lunch, the boys put a blindfold over Charlotte's eyes and led her down to the barn. They placed the end of a halter in her hand and then removed the blindfold. At the other end of the halter was a beautiful white Arab stallion.

"Happy birthday, Mother," they sang.

She was thirty-seven that day. She threw her arms round each of them in turn and then she threw her arms round the neck of the stallion and burst into a flood of tears.

She called the horse Trojan.

Chapter Seventeen

"Where are they all rushing to?" Charlotte wondered. "Dear me, I must be really from the sticks now."

The buzz of Dallas was making her quite giddy. The cab drew up in front of the hotel. The towering dark glass edifice reflected the bustle and life of the city. Connie was waiting for her in the fashionable foyer.

"Charlotte," she gushed, as they hugged each other. Connie was exquisitely dressed and groomed as befitted the Queen Bee of Dallas society, which she now was. All the other sophisticated and beautifully dressed and superbly groomed women greeted her as she steered Charlotte to a quiet corner of the terrace where a table had been reserved for them.

Charlotte had heard nothing from her friend since they had parted in Edinburgh. She missed Beaumont not at all. True, there was little time to think back on the days of social whirl, and even less inclination. She did send Christmas cards to a few of those to whom she had been closest. Connie was among them. It was a great surprise when the phone call came from Connie in Dallas with the invitation, and now here they were, meeting for the first time since Edinburgh.

"It is lovely to see you again, Charlotte, and you have such an air of self-confidence about you. You look the soul of contentment."

"And well I might, because I have every reason to be content. I have never been happier, Connie."

"Charlotte, I just can't believe it. The last place on earth I ever dreamed of seeing you would be on a ranch. You were such a town bird. How on earth did it ever come about? I just lost track of you completely. Oh, our little circle in Beumont was awash with speculation. We did hear from Bibi Morgenstern that you had bought her niece's ranch somewhere up around Amarillo. I confess, Charlotte that I didn't even know Amarillo was in Texas. It could have been next door to Timbuktu for all I knew. A ranch - I just could not believe it! I mean, all those cows and horses and open spaces, it just isn't you somehow."

111

"Well, Connie it is me now and very much me."

"I know, Darling, but do tell me - how did it ever come about? I just cannot imagine it."

"Oh, it is a long long story, but I'll give you the bare bones. As you know, Tom joined me in Edinburgh. Well, we went for a journey through the Highlands of Scotland. It took about four weeks. It is very hard to explain. It wasn't just a journey of discovery of the Highlands. We were undergoing a journey of self-discovery too. Our marriage was on the rocks. We hadn't realised just how far apart we had grown. We also discovered that that was the last thing we wanted. It was a kind of catharsis. I can't imagine it ever happening anywhere other than the Highlands. It is a land of magic.

"Well, we came back to the States on the QE2. By that time we had decided that Beaumont was no longer what we needed in our lives. In our newfound truthful relationship I discovered that Tom had always wanted a ranch. I liked the idea too. We went to fetch the boys from camp in Vermont and we took a journey through part of the States. The boys wanted to see 'the other end of Texas' as they put it. We spent a night in a motel in a little place called San Miguel. It is not too far from Amarillo. The boys took a great interest in the rural parts of the |States. We had never relaised before that this interest was there. Well, we went to a rodeo and I guess that was us hooked. I am sure fate took a hand in matters. I'll tell you about it sometime. I just can't find any other explanation for those events.

"The boys met young ranchers of their own age at the rodeo and they struck up an immediate friendship and that was it. Those young men knew of a ranch that was coming up for sale and they took our boys to see it and that was that. We live there now. I can't imagine living anywhere else. As I said, we are all very happy there."

"And it shows, but can I just take you to task a teeny little bit?"

"Sure, Connie. I guess that's what you are going to do anyway."

"I know it isn't so important out there on a ranch, but you mustn't let yourself go too much to seed. You are becoming positively plump, Charlotte, and at your age it is not so easy to get the weight off again."

"Oh, Connie, I shall be all right. Don't worry. I shall be shedding this particular extra weight in about four months' time."

"Charlotte, you're not … you're not pregnant again?"

"Yes, I am Connie. That was another of the happenings."

There was a silence. A curious expression crossed Connie's face. Just for a moment Charlotte thought she saw envy.

"But how lovely for you, Darling. Now, you must take great care of yourself from now on."

"Not much chance of doing anything else. Tom treats me like I was bone china and the boys would wrap me up in eiderdown if they got the chance. You should have heard the fuss the first day I went riding."

"You didn't go riding in your condition, Charlotte!"

"Of course I did."

"That was very irresponsible of you."

"My foot, Connie! Women have been known to go riding after they have fallen pregnant. In fact, there are stories of women giving birth in the saddle. Mind you I think that is a bit far-fetched. By the way, would you like to be godmother to the child when it arrives?"

Connie sniffled and then dabbed at her eyes.

"Why, Charlotte, I am just so touched. I will be honoured to be the child's godmother and I am joining the others in telling you to be more careful. I have a personal interest now. If anything should befall that child, I shall … I shall … well, there will be hell to pay, Charlotte Benson."

Charlotte smiled.

"But that is enough of my story. Tell me how you came to be in Dallas."

"There isn't much to tell. When your Tom suddenly changed tack and sold out to the cartel it took them all by surprise. They felt they had been taken to the cleaners in a way. They paid well over the odds. They were really sore about it for quite a while. In a way they blamed my Bob and so he got the means together somehow and bought them out. Within two weeks they discovered oil in one of the areas, which had not looked very promising. Well, the oil just gushed and then there was a dramatic upturn in oil prices and Bob was king of the heap. The dollars just poured in and the others in the cartel were more than ever sore. Anyway, Bob was now a major player in the field, and living in Beaumont was no longer an option. All the business was in Dallas and so we moved here and the dollars rolled in even faster. Poor Bob, he was working his b … He worked very hard. It was all too much for him. He got an ulcer and then one morning at breakfast he clutched his chest and that was it. He was dead before the medics arrived.

"Well to cut a long story short, all the dollars came my way. I am President of the Corporation, but I take very little to do with it. I just get on with my 'social whirl' as you used to call it. I employ people to run it, mostly the husbands of those women you see around here. I know they think I'm from Hicksville, but since they all work for or with my Corporation they have to be sweet to me and I don't mind one little bit."

"You've done very well, Connie. I am just so pleased for you. You must be really wealthy now."

"I'm rolling in it, Charlotte, but that doesn't mean all that much to me. Do you know, Charlotte, the nicest thing to happen to me for a long time, and the thing that means most to me, is being asked to be godmother to your child when it arrives; that and your visit. And, Charlotte, I am telling you right now, you be very careful how you go. If anything happens to that child I'll never forgive you."

Connie's concern was in vain. Charlotte continued to ride as her girth increased. She formed a great attachment to Trojan. She rode out over the range almost every day and even her increasing girth did not deter her. She was out on the range when her labour pains started. She rode back as carefully and quickly as she could. Fortunately Tom was by the barn when she got back. He led the horse back up to the house and took her down from the saddle and with only Trojan looking on he delivered the baby girl right there on the verandah.

She was born exactly nine months and two weeks from the day Tom had arrived in Scotland.

"What shall we call her?" asked Tom. "I think she should have a Highland name with a pedigree like she has, conceived in Scotland and born in Texas. Pedigrees don't come better than that."

"Yes, a Highland name would be nice. Have you any ideas?"

"Not really. Do you remember that very nice girl we met on Barra, you know the one who taught us the dance steps. Her name was Rhona. I have always liked the name since then."

"Yes, it is a lovely name. Rhona it will be then."

"Yes, she was a very spirited and lovely girl. Maybe this one will grow up to be just as beautiful and spirited."

Lady Lomond was wrong in one of her predictions. It was almost two years before Tom got round to indulging himself in his hobby of the study of history. By that time there was a raven-haired little girl with large intense blue eyes running around the house. She was universally adored and she was totally devoted to Tom and followed him everywhere.

Chapter Eighteen

Angus was an apt pupil. That first day, he had needed a long soak in a hot bath and a liberal rubbing of alcohol to rid him of saddle soreness. He had got over that now and within three days he was able to separate out a steer, rope it and mark it. Rhona was thrilled with his progress. They were constantly on horseback.

He came out from his shower looking clean and scrubbed and very fit. The wide-legged gait was a thing of the past. Charlotte got up and poured him a drink and brought it to him where he stood on the edge of the verandah.

"I just can't seem to get enough of this superb country. It just gets to you."

"I'm very happy to hear that, Angus; but, you know, it is hard work. Don't let Rhona work you too hard."

"Not a chance of that, Mom. Angus has stamina you wouldn't believe and he is as strong as any horse."

"Well, don't work him too hard. It is supposed to be something of a holiday for him too. I'll see to supper," said Charlotte.

"Oh no, Mom. You sit right there. I'll get supper," Rhona insisted.

"I'll help you," Angus offered.

"You do realise it involves more than just roasting a hunk of meat on the fire at the mouth of a cave. In the States we have all kinds of gadgets now."

"Another remark like that and I shall club you over the head to show my affection for you and drag you to the kitchen by your hair."

"It looks like they are getting on like a house on fire," thought Charlotte.

They continued to tease each other and there was much fun. Every now and then great gales of laughter came from the kitchen. The supper they placed on the table was quite delectable.

"I think we have another cowboy on our hands, Mom. This guy is coming on real fast. I think he is a natural."

"Why, that's just fine," said Charlotte.

"I have the best of teachers. I couldn't have better I am sure, and besides I am in training for the rodeo."

"Ah yes, Mom, he's been pestering me to tell him all about the rodeo. I said for him to wait and that you would tell him about the rodeo. I told him you are the expert in rodeo in these parts."

"Now that is pure exaggeration. Don't pay her no heed."

"Not so, Angus. You ask Ben or any of his cronies. They'll tell you with pride just how Mom rescued the rodeo event, which was all but dead on its feet, and made it into the best event of the year in San Miguel. Anyway, do tell Angus about the rodeo. He might just change his mind about taking part when he knows what it is all about."

"Well, if you would be so kind as to fetch the coffee, I'll tell Angus all about it."

Despite her protestations, Charlotte was an expert on rodeo. That first rodeo had made a very deep and lasting impression on her. Not only that, but she felt a sense of obligation to the event. That, more than anything, had decided the boys that ranching was to be their life, and for that Charlotte would always feel grateful. When the man who had been the driving force in organising the event passed away, no one seemed very keen to take up the reins and in two short years the event had   all but gone. There was talk of giving up the rodeo completely.

Charlotte was horrified when she heard of the proposal. She nagged, persuaded, cajoled and threatened any one who would listen. Tom and Ben were the main targets of her concern. It was Ben who, in a moment of frustration, dared her to take on the job herself. She rose to the challenge. She read everything she could lay hands on about rodeo, the history and the events, and she attended every rodeo within a hundred miles. The result of all that was that the San Miguel rodeo became the top rodeo event for a hundred miles around and even further afield and Charlotte became a recognised authority on the subject.

"A rodeo is basically a competition involving the skills of the cowboy. Many have tried new events and gimmicks over the years, but the basics have fortunately survived," she told Angus.

"Rodeo comes from the Spanish word, 'rodear', which means to encircle or to surround. To the Spanish in New Spain - now Mexico - in the mid-sixteenth century, a rodeo was simply a cattle roundup. It is probably inevitable that a competitive and flashy culmination to these roundups would evolve: it was a chance for cowhands to show off their skills in breaking an especially wild bronco or flaunt their flair as a roper. But it wasn't until the mid-eighteen hundreds that these contests got organized into full-fledged celebrations. Texas would like to take credit for the first rodeo celebration. In the early eighteen eighties, in the West Texas town of Pecos, cowboys would get off work and come into town on the Fourth of July, also known as 'Cowboy Christmas'. They would thunder down Main Street, roping steers and corralling the critters in the courthouse square. By some historical accounts, this was the birth of rodeo. Even though Coloradoans also claim that distinction, Texans did have something to do with one of the earliest rodeos, this one in Cheyenne, Wyoming, in Eighteen Seventy-two. The occasion was the forerunner of the weeklong Frontier Days still held in Cheyenne. As the story goes, a group of Texas cowboys arrived in Cheyenne and decided to celebrate July Fourth with an exhibition of their steer-riding prowess. The event must have been successful, because the next year local cowboys chose to do a little bronco busting to celebrate Independence Day, down the middle of one of Cheyenne's main streets. Bronco-busting a hundred years ago didn't have the advantage of a life-saving buzzer going off after eight seconds - cowboys rode the bronco until either it or the rider gave out, and sometimes that was as long as twenty minutes.

"Rodeos emerged from the workaday world of the cowboy along with America's growing fascination with the West. In Eighteen eighty-two, Buffalo Bill Cody turned the West into lucrative entertainment with his first Wild West show. Cody used the term 'rodeo' for these extravaganzas, which included roping, riding, bronco busting, and bull riding - always the thrilling finale. Sometimes, as many as a thousand cowboys competed for prizes. By the Eighteen nineties, rodeos were commonplace all over the cattle-raising regions of the West. Nowadays, the rodeo has shifted away from its origins as a way for working cowboys to blow off steam; it is more of a show, and demands all the time and money a major theatrical production might cost. An aspiring cowboy or cowgirl will have to compete in eighty to a hundred and twenty-five rodeos a year, be well-subsidized - thousands and thousands of dollars can be spent on travel and entry fees alone, not to mention horses, equipment, and maintenance - and expect to spend at least two hundred days a year on the road.

"But, Angus, ranch rodeos are the real thing. If you want to see how cowboys really work, day in and day out, watch these events.

Ranch rodeos are competitions between ranches and are not part of the Professional Rodeo Cowboys' Association circuit. They tend to be more modest affairs, in small arenas, in small towns, but they maintain an authenticity that gives them an appeal that the PRCA rodeos can't achieve. That is the kind of rodeo we have here. I shall never forget that first rodeo I saw in San Miguel. We were all hooked from the word go. We had been thinking in terms of a ranch. After seeing that rodeo, we were convinced."

"I can well imagine. Just how is the Ranch Rodeo different?"

"The team work and the events basically. The events are Bronc Riding, where one rider represents each ranch participating in the rodeo in this timed event. They ride, using a stock saddle, until either the horse throws them or the buzzer sounds.

Then there is Sorting, where a team of five cowboys works to remove cows from a herd in a specific numerical order. As the riders cross the starting line, the announcer calls a number; while four cowboys hold the herd, the fifth must cut out each cow from the herd in the order called. This is a timed event.

"After that comes Team Roping. The objective in this timed event is to cut a designated animal from a herd, head it, and then heel it, which means tie up its front legs and then with the same rope secure its hind legs. Then comes Team Doctoring. A roper must cut away from a herd of yearlings, weighing about five hundred and fifty pounds each, a designated animal, drive it and rope it while a second cowboy heels the animal. A cowboy, designated as the veterinarian, dismounts and draws a chalk mark between the yearling's eyes. The lowest time wins.

"The star of the show is the Wild Cow Milking. That is always considered the most hilarious of the rodeo events. Wild cow milking involves all members of a team. One rider ropes the cow while another milks her. Any of the four team members can run to the judges' booth with the milk."

"Yes, I can see that would involve quite a bit of hilarity."

"It does at that, and then they get on to Branding. This is the real work-a-day cowboy's event. It is a timed event in which a roper crosses a start line and enters a herd of cattle. He ropes a calf and moves it across the line where his teammates position the calf on its side and remove the rope. This is the signal for the brander to leave his designated area and race over to the calf to apply the brand. Once branding is completed, the brander returns to his area and timing ceases.

"The last event on the list is Team Penning. Here cowboys work together in this timed event to see which team can cut three designated calves from a herd of numbered calves and move them to a pen across the arena. The lowest time wins, and that basically is what a rodeo is about."

"I just can't wait to see that. Does the Lone Pine Ranch have a team in the events?"

"Of course. I think our cowboys can hold their own with any ranch. Everyone says they are the team to beat. Do you think you could take part in any of those events?"

"Not a hope in Hades, but I think I shall just carry on with improving my skills and learning what I can from my expert teacher."

"Yes! She is good, isn't she?"

"Is some one talking about me?"

Rhona's voice cut into the conversation.

"We were just saying how good you are," said Charlotte.

"Well, thanks. Angus is good too, Mom, real good, and he puts so much into it."

"Why that's just fine," Charlotte remarked. "I am happy to hear just how well you are doing, Angus. It says lot for both of you, but Rhona, you must make sure Angus has some fun too. I'd hate to think he went back to Scotland with the impression that all we do is work. They have a lot of fun in Scotland, you know."

"Yeah! I guess you are right. We'll ride over to see Ben and Mary Alice after tea. The kids will be back home tomorrow night, anyway. Kelly is bound to want to hog Angus all to herself and we may not get the chance."

"Sounds good to me," he said.

There was a full moon rising just behind the lone pine tree. It was a great deep-golden orb in the still night sky.

"What a beautiful sight," said Angus. "Even the moon is bigger in Texas. How do you ever manage that? And it is a deeper shade of gold. You know, with that lone pine just there in the picture, that is the backdrop for a musical. Shall I sing to you Rhona?"

"Sure! Who am I to spoil a romantic moment; but could I suggest we saddle up and hit the trail while we are about it?"

"I think maybe we are just a shade more romantic in the Highlands."

Charlotte watched them as they rode off down the road. Angus now sat in the saddle with complete ease. The rising moon bathed the landscape in a soft silvery light. It lent a mystic quality to the open range.

"No wonder Angus is impressed. With his Celtic blood comes a good deal of romanticism. The brush and the mesquite are just as romantic to him as were the heather and the thistle to Tom and me," she thought.

Chapter Nineteen

They got a great welcome from the Fergusons. The family came out to greet them as they dismounted. Ben kissed Rhona.

"How is my favourite girl tonight?"

"Just fine, Ben, and how is my favourite man?"

"Pretty good, but just a little concerned over how long I am going to remain your favourite man."

"That you will always be, Ben, no matter what happens. Come meet Angus."

Ben shook his hand warmly and then stood back.

"So, it is all true. You are as big as they said you were. You are very welcome. Come meet Mary Alice."

"That will be my pleasure."

"Why you are just as big and handsome as they said you were and you are as welcome as can be and do you know I am goin' to give you a big hug and a kiss?"

She put her arms round Angus and kissed him warmly on the cheek.

"Watch out, Angus. She has a reputation in these parts," said Ben

"Well, come on inside and have a drink," said Mary Alice.

"Aw, gee, no Mom, not just yet. We want to see Angus perform with some of his heavyweight events."

Mary Alice looked at Angus. He just shrugged his shoulders.

"Well, you have ten minutes, not one second more."

"Is it true that you are champion hammer-thrower of the Highlands?"

"No, that's my father. I am very small beer where heavyweight athletics are concerned. Anyway, you seem pretty well informed about my activities back home. How come?"

"Oh, we have had Andrew Leslie visit us. He's one of your biggest fans. After what he told us, we just couldn't wait for you to visit. We got one or two things together. We kinda hoped you might give us a demonstration, perhaps."

"The thing is, Angus, our Charlie fancies himself as a bit of a strong man and he just wants to see how he measures up," said Sam.

"Probably very well from the looks of him," said Angus.

It was almost half-an-hour later that Mary Alice came out to where they were.

"Oh, oh," said Charlie. "I think we'd better stop there. Ma looks like she's got her feathers all ruffled; but, Angus, thanks a lot. That was great. I really appreciate that."

Mary Alice took Angus by an arm and led him indoors without a word.

She saw the two riders approach along the moonlit track. They rode close together and often they looked towards each other.

"What a lovely picture they make," she thought. "A handsome young man and an attractive vivacious young woman out riding in the moonlight."

Charlotte watched him dismount. He did so with an easy grace. He stretched up and lifted Rhona from the saddle. His arm was loosely round her when they came out of the stables.

"Can I get you a drink - perhaps a Texas Bourbon? It will be a change from Scotch," said Charlotte when they had settled on the verandah.

"I would love a Texas Bourbon and, thank you, but with a lot of water. Bourbon is just that bit stronger than our whisky," said Hector.

Charlotte poured generous Bourbon and added a good measure of ice-cold water.

On impulse she poured Bourbon for herself. She quite often used to join Tom in a nightcap. Since he died she had lost the habit.

"I think I need this anyway. There is so much that I have to come to terms with, " she thought.

"Would you like a drink Rhona?" she asked

"I'll take a Coke. It's all right, I'll get it."

She went off to the fridge to get her Coke and Charlotte settled down where the old fig tree cast its shadow. She felt a sense of comfort sitting in the shadow. She watched the big young man as he sipped his drink. He stretched like a big cat. He was a relaxed and happy man.

"How like his father he is," she thought again. "I wonder what happened to Hector? I wonder if I shall ever find out."

"I always thought that every one was called 'Mac something' in the Highlands," said Rhona when she joined them, "but now I see that isn't so. There is Andrew Leslie and he isn't Mac anything."

"No, not all. Most clans begin with 'Mac', but there are others like Leslie and Graham."

"Mom often comes out with some of the most outlandish tales of the Highlands. I often wonder what is true and what is legend."

"That isn't all that easy, even for a Highlander. Quite often the line between fact and fancy is pretty well blurred, as it is in our clan. I could tell you a wee story, but you'd probably find it boring."

"I'm sure it won't be," said Charlotte.

"Yeah. I've told you a lot of legends of Texas, so come on, Angus, you owe me a legend or two," said Rhona.

"Well, here goes. Stop me if it does get boring."

"My family comes from Nether Lorne now, but we originated a bit to the south in the Knapdale and Tarbert area. We are descended from one Alan nan Sop - Alan of the straws. He lived in that area in the mid-fourteen hundreds and led a band of men and they plundered, robbed, raped and pillaged their way around what is now Argyll and even over to the Clyde estuary. It is not quite as bad as it sounds. That was pretty well par for the course in those days. Alan nan Sop and his gang just did it better than most. Perhaps they were that bit more ruthless.

"Now Alan, according to legend, got his name from the circumstances surrounding his birth, which were rather unusual. When his mother was carrying him she offended an old witch who put a spell on her. The witch told her that she would never be delivered of the child she was carrying and it appeared that was to be the case. The poor woman carried the child for almost eighteen months until the baby grew so big that she could no longer go on. By some ruse they diverted the attention of the witch just long enough for the woman to be delivered of the child. She was on her way to her own home to have the child, but had only got halfway there when her pains started. Those attending her spread out a bed of straw for her to lie on and the baby was delivered right there. It is said that as soon as he was born he grabbed a handful of straw and took a great bite out of the middle of it.

"That is purely legend, of course. No one in his right senses would ever think otherwise. However, it is a fact that the Maclean wives tend to carry their babies for longer than normal. It has been known for them to carry their children for almost ten months. The strange thing is that this trait is passed on down the male line, and it does happen in our family too."

Charlotte ceased to breath. She closed her eyes tight to try to escape, but there was no escape. In that instant she knew what had been bothering her. Quite suddenly the nebulous thoughts, which had eluded her, crystalised. The realisation made her gasp. She drew a long rasping breath and closed her eyes tight.

"Oh, my God, oh my God, oh Tom," she cried into herself. "Oh Tom, what shall I do?" she whispered.

Yes, it was the eyes. She saw again Rhona's intense blue eyes and her dark hair. She had always assumed that those traits had been inherited from Tom's Irish Celtic ancestors. In that instant, however, she knew that the genes of Hector Maclean passed on the intense blue eyes and the raven hair.

"Oh, I should have seen it. I almost did. Oh God, what am I to do? What am I to do?"

She sat silent for a while. She didn't dare to think lest more devastation should befall her mind. At last she opened her eyes. She blessed the fact that she sat in the shade. They would not have noticed her deathly pallor. Thankfully, they appeared unaware of the mayhem and devastation, which had befallen her. Slowly and deeply she breathed to regain her composure.

"Why, that's a great story. The Highlands of Scotland must be a fascinating place," said Rhona.

"It's all of that, and beautiful with it," said Charlotte. She was glad her voice had not betrayed her emotion.

"I think I shall go down and have a look at Trojan before I turn in. I thought he was a little off colour today."

"I'll come with you," volunteered Angus.

"That's kind of you, but no thanks. I think he'd prefer me to be on my own."

"Mom dotes on that horse, Angus. He's the most mollycoddled animal I've ever seen."

"That's not quite true. He was a birthday present from the boys the first birthday I spent on the ranch. He was quite young then. We kind of matured together. It is only natural if I have a strong affection for him."

"And a very fine thing too," said Angus. "I have never had a lot to do with horses, but since coming to Texas I can understand any one being attached to them. They are wonderful animals."

Charlotte walked quite slowly down to the barn. She had to resist a strong impulse to flee into the night. She whistled and Trojan was there at the paddock gate to meet her. She threw her arms round his neck. He sensed her discomposure. She felt his chin rub her back and then he raised his head and she felt his velvet lips on her cheek.

"Dear Trojan. What am I to do? I have no idea."

Her arms were round Trojan's neck and her head nestled against him. She was silent for a long time whilst she marshaled her thoughts.

"I'll sleep on it. My mind will be clearer in the morning. I shall ride out to the lone pine and talk with Tom. Yes, that's what I'll do. Things are always better when I've talked with Tom. Good night, dear Trojan."

She kissed him on the cheek and walked slowly back towards the house. She was deep in thought.

"I wonder what became of Hector?"

Hector

"Now you, Hector, are becoming a first class athlete, but you are not enough of a showman," said Duncan Maclvor. "You will have to pay more attention to that aspect. We need to pay more attention to the showman side of things, you know. We have to provide entertainment too. The more people and tourists who attend, the better the prize money."

"That's right," assented the others.

"But why me in particular?" asked Hector.

"Because, my wee boy" said Andy Campbell, "you are the biggest, strongest and most spectacular of the lot of us. Damn your eyes."

There was a burst of laughter.

Hector had his first year at university behind him and was again on the Highland Games circuit. He was having a drink with the others at the end of the first games of the season. He drank very moderately and he loved the camaraderie of his friends and competitors.

"Oh, well, all right. I'm game for anything."

It was Duncan Maclvor who played the biggest part in his training.

"If we go about things right, you will have the P.R. men on your heels in no time. There is good money in that," advised Duncan. "But watch out for those photographers. They are not beyond slipping a hand up your kilt. Mind you, that can be a rewarding experience too."

Hector was never quite sure when Duncan was teasing. The advertising men approached him in early August. They took his training in hand and his likeness graced many a tourist pamphlet and Highland product. He quickly became a consummate showman.

They all sat under a tree waiting for the Earl to present the prizes. The Chairman of the organising committee was giving his usual speech and thanking all and sundry.

"I know what I would be saying if I had that microphone in my hand right now," said Andy Campbell.

"What's that?" asked Duncan MacIvor.

"I'd say, would big Hecky Maclean come forward and collect his usual lion's share of the loot. That was not the best of ideas we had two years ago, because since then the big bugger has grabbed the lion's share of the publicity, the best of the prizes and the best of the crumpet. Now, I do not wish him any harm, but it will give the rest of us half a chance if he were to break a leg about the beginning of July next year. Mother Nature has been a bit over-liberal with him, anyway; he has had more than his share of beauty, brains and balls."

The loud guffaws almost drowned out the speech from the platform.

"It's all right, Andy. The field is yours next year. I shan't be there. I finish at Uni next year and I shall have to look for proper work."

"You know," said Andy, "we shall miss you, you big bugger, and I really mean that."

At the end of the final year, the University held a seminar to introduce graduates to prospective employers. Hector received many offers and chose a Multinational, which offered him the chance to work abroad.

Chapter Twenty

Charlotte let the reins go loose and the big white Arab stallion turned his head towards the pine tree. She no longer needed to guide him He knew where they were going. This was Charlotte's favourite spot in all of the world. It was a spot, which held dear, sweet memories for her. Today she let Trojan find his own way. She was deep in thought. She slipped from the saddle and tied Trojan loosely to the rail under the tree. He nuzzled her affectionately under the chin. She stroked his ears and took a lump of sugar from her pocket. His lips were velvet smooth as he took it gently from her palm and then he dropped his head and began munching grass.

Charlotte sat down on the seat he had put there so many years ago. This was their own special place. Not even the children were encouraged to come here. The big pine tree gave a welcome shade. She always felt closer to Tom here. It was mostly here that she talked to Tom.

"What now, my love? Where do we go from here? Should I have seen much sooner that Hector was her natural father? It was the timing that threw me. I remember counting the days when she came near to being born. I needed all your reassurance then, Tom, and I think I was relieved when nine months from the day you arrived in Scotland had passed. I was glad for you, Tom, when a day grew to a week and one week to two. I had not counted on the legend of Alan nan Sop. Yes, Tom, like so many other things in the Highlands, it is not just legend."

She looked out over the dry and dusty range. The ranch house could be seen in the distance. It was a happy, contented house sitting there on its own little hillock, she mused; and then, quite suddenly, the thought came into her head and its sudden realisation rocked her anew.

"You knew, Tom. All this time you knew. I know now that you did. I think I know just how you came to know as well, and I know why. I remember the words you used: 'If ever I can do anything for him I shall do it.' And you did. What better than to bring up his daughter in the way you have? She is a credit to your upbringing. I always knew you were a good man. I think you were also great. Oh,

Tom, you knew she was not of your flesh. You met the brothers at Braemar. I remember how well you described them - the big men who loved life and whisky. Yes, they had black black hair and blue blue eyes. Now that I know, I see the strong resemblance between her and Angus. I should have seen it right away. And yet she was your daughter. She was more your daughter than she is mine. I suspect she will always be. I shall not tell your daughter unless I have to, Tom. Oh, Tom, did I love him? Well just a little bit - rather like the way I love my sons. It was not the way I love you. No one will ever replace you in my heart. Not now. Not ever. I love you."

She always felt better when he had talked to Tom. Now she felt more able to cope with what might come. For a moment, she regretted the years in which she had not recognised his greatness, the years when she did not give him the chance; but then she began counting blessings. She thought over the years on the ranch. She remembered the first time the Rhona sat on a horse.

Charlotte lay back in the lounger and watched Tom as he placed Rhona in the saddle. She was now just three months past her second birthday. The last three months had seen tantrums, cajoling and sulks, and now she was, for the first time, being allowed to sit in the saddle and and ride the new pony. This was her birthday present from her brothers. He was a smart little piebald pony with a long flowing mane. Charlotte could recall the ecstatic Rhona's face when she saw the pony on the morning of her birthday. Neither she nor Tom had any warning. The boys had bought the pony with their own money and without telling anyone. They wanted to sit Rhona on the pony right away. It was Connie who refused to allow that.

"Rhona is my God child and I will just not allow it. She is only two, for God's sake, Charlotte."

Connie did take her duties as Godmother very seriously. She insisted on coming to the ranch for Rhona's birthday party and she arrived with a mountain of parcels containing pretty dresses and soft toys and children's books. She also deposited a generous amount of money in the bank account she had opened for Rhona on the day she was born. The boys good-naturedly gave in. They adored Aunt Connie and she never failed to remember their birthdays either. Charlotte drank her iced tea and watched Tom with admiration. How patient he was and how understanding. It wasn't just with Rhona, he was equally understanding with the older ones too. How quickly time had flown. Sometimes it seemed as though ranching had always been their life. Beaumont with its social whirl was light years away. She very seldom thought about those days now and never with any regret. She shifted her weight; the baby was due any day now. I sort of hope it will be a girl. Rhona is a bit outnumbered.

Just occasionally Charlotte had doubts about the involvement of all of the family in ranching.

"Maybe we might get just a bit insular, Tom," she said.

"You could be insular in a much worse way of life. We have freedom and healthy living and a good clean, decent lifestyle ... and, do you know, it is very profitable too?"

"I suppose you are right," she said.

Charlotte insisted that they pay a visit to Dallas or Huston two or three times a year. They visited galleries and museums and attended concerts and the ballet. The boys took a polite interest in culture, but Charlotte was quite sure they were very relieved to get back to the ranch.

Just occasionally she went on her own to spend a day or two with Connie. She allowed herself a little break soon after Kelly's first birthday.

They were having a martini before lunch. Connie insisted on spoiling Charlotte whenever she came to Dallas.

"Now tell me how Mike and Liz are settling down. I haven't seen you since the wedding. Oh what a beautiful wedding that was."

"Is that the last time I saw you, Connie? Goodness, time does fly. That was nearly six months ago. Well, they are settling down just fine. With a bit of help from Tom and a bit from Ben, they managed to buy the ranch without going for a loan."

"But, Charlotte, I would have bought that ranch for them. I wouldn't even have missed the money."

"That's kind of you, Connie, but that wouldn't have gone down well. We could have bought it for them, too, but they wouldn't have gone along with that either. We eventually did manage to persuade them to let us help a little. It went a bit against the grain at the time. They wanted to do everything on their own. However, Tom managed to persuade them. It was a bit like something out of Africa, getting all those cattle as wedding presents. Now for the good news, Connie - we are going to become grandparents."

"How lovely. Oh, I am just so thrilled for them and for you too. What a fine young couple they are. And they are right too. They will get much more satisfaction doing things in their own way. I'm just so proud of them."

"Well, I'd better get all the surprises over with. You see..."

"I know what you are about to say, Charlotte. You too are pregnant."

"How did you guess?"

"I suspected as soon as I saw you coming down the stairs. You get a kind of glow when you are pregnant, a kind of air of contentment."

"Yes, I suppose I do."

"This is for the sixth time and, Charlotte, you are over forty."

"I know, Connie. It is just that Tom and I discovered, really discovered each other so late in life that we are making the best of it. I think this will be the last, though."

Charlotte glanced over to her friend. There was a strange faraway look on her face.

"I envy you in many ways, Charlotte. You have all the things that matter right around you."

"Yes, I suppose I have; but you have a good life, too, here in Dallas. You are queen bee. You are top of the heap where the social scene is concerned. Don't you enjoy it."

"Oh, sure I do - even the bitchiness. Come to think of it, I think I enjoy the bitchiness as much as anything else about this scene. There are so many women here who are just so sweet to your face and you know quite well they would love to unseat you and take over your pitch, but they can't; not with my dollars they can't, and so they just have to smile sweetly and wait in the wings. But I find myself day-dreaming more and more. I often wonder what would have happened if I had met my road to Damascus the way you did. I often think, well you have the family life and everything that goes with it, the sex life, the children, everything. I often wonder what that would be like."

Charlotte looked at her friend and somehow she felt a great sympathy for her. This was not the frivolous Connie of old. She too had matured.

"You're mellowing, dear Connie," she said.

"I guess I am, and with it comes this introspection and not a little of nostalgia. I remember that trip we took. God, I was foolish in those days."

"Not really, Connie."

"Oh, I was, Charlotte. I was just so insecure and had a lot of bravado to cover it up. I remember the night I went for a walk along the Bonnie Banks of Loch Lomond with that big Highlander. That was sheer bravado. I had to prove that I wasn't scared to go walking on my own with a man. He was dressed the way Highlanders are supposed to dress and he sat on a rock in a way that made sure I saw that too. He was a well-made guy. Charlotte, I took to my heels and ran all the way back to the hotel."

Charlotte threw back her head and laughed.

Charlotte's sixth child was born on the same day as her first grandson. There was a joint christening three months later and Connie was the proud Godmother to both children.

Chapter Twenty-One

The organ music rang triumphantly through the packed little church. Some of the guests had had to stand in the aisles during the ceremony and now the lovely bride and the proud groom led the congregation out into the bright Texan sunshine. Charlotte's heart swelled with pride. Time for Tom and her was now measured in weddings and birthdays. She was becoming accustomed to weddings. This was their third in two years and this one had an added thrill for Charlotte. As the bride swept past, Charlotte's eyes rested fondly on the flower girl. Her black hair hung in ringlets and the large blue blue eyes lit up as they met Charlotte's.

"Yes. Our daughter is a beautiful child," thought Charlotte. She turned to Tom. He too was looking at Rhona and the expression in his eyes spoke of love and pride and achievement.

It seemed that their sons were leaving the home with almost indecent haste. One day they were awkward gangling high school adolescents and the next they had filled out physically and become mature young men with lovely girls on their arms, and quite suddenly they were adults making their own way in the world. Charlotte looked beyond Tom to her oldest son, Mike. He cradled their first grandson in his arms as he watched the wedding procession and beyond him Bob had his arm round his wife Louisa. Their first child was due quite soon. Amy and Gary, the bride and groom, were going to follow the example of his older brothers. They too were going to take up ranching in the county.

"More and more I tend to forget that we have ever had any life beyond San Miguel County," thought Charlotte.

Tom had taken to ranching with a zeal that surprised even Charlotte. Ben and Mary Alice had shown a keen interest in their neighbours from the start. They were always there with a helping hand and a word of advice when it was needed. Tom had read every book on ranching and cattle raising that he could find. He soon got a feel for ranching and success quickly followed. It was Ben who gave him the greatest accolade.

"Don't know too much of what Tom did before, but whatever it was he was wasting his time. He is a fine rancher. He has grown into this job faster than any man I ever did see. I'm durned of he isn't showing me how to ranch now."

She sat there and continued to indulge herself in memories. They were happy memories. They were memories of the years of achievement and contentment they had had since they moved to the ranch. She thought of all the hard work they had put into the ranch and how the boys had loved it so. She remembered the first ride she and Tom took to the lone pine tree. That was after she had convinced them all that it was safe for her to ride. She had had to work hard to make them understand. She acquitted herself well on a horse. The riding lessons, which she had had as a girl, were now proving to be very useful, but since she had fallen pregnant Tom treated her as though she was made of delicate china.

Dear Tom. He was never far from her thoughts. He was a wonderful husband and lover. He was a wonderful father and he was a wonderful man. He found time for his work and his family. He even found time to become an authority on the history of San Antonio and he was frequently asked to lecture at the university there. Just now and then Charlotte had pangs of regret that she had not spent more time with the boys as they grew up. She made amends with Rhona, but she too seemed to grow with indecent haste. The burden of bringing up Rhona fell on Tom. Rhona was only four when little Tom was born. In those early years, a bond was formed between Rhona and Tom that grew stronger with each passing year.

As the families grew and the numbers assembling for Sunday lunch and Thanksgiving and Christmas weekends grew ever larger, they knew that the old ranch house had to grow too. This expansion was in character and now the house had expanded into a big roomy and comfortable place with pantiles and cool archways and patios in the Old Spanish style. It was above all a house where children could roam free. Four or five times a year they invited their friends and neighbours for dinner. The old house was bursting at the seams on those occasions. Mary Alice and Ben Ferguson had remained their dearest friends from the time they came to San Miguel. Ben watched the growth in their clan with increasing satisfaction.

"You will soon have to grow a long white beard, Tom, as befits a patriarch," he teased.

It was just two years ago that they brought his body in from the range. Ben Ferguson came along with them. The horse had stumbled in an ants' nest and he had been thrown from the saddle. His neck was broken. He had died instantly. Charlotte herself died a little at that time. Ben held her close. There was comfort in the smell of tobacco smoke that clung to his clothes.

"You will grieve for him. That is natural, but don't grieve too much. Tom Benson had what is denied to most men. He was the most contented man I ever knew. He died without pain and he died without envy. He died with a sense of achievement and he died with peace and contentment in his heart. That is not given to many men."

"I know, but I shall miss him dreadfully."

"I know what he was to you. Keep all that in your heart and you will never go wrong. Meantime, you have his children to care for."

The town closed down on the day of his burial. The service was held in the church there and then he was laid to rest with only the family and Ben in attendance. Rhona felt his loss more than any one. She spoke hardly at all. She went about the business of looking after the ranch just as Tom had so patiently taught her, and Charlotte's heart ached for her.

"What am I to do, Ben?" she asked.

"I don't rightly know. Sit on it for a few days. The answer will come of its own accord."

They came on Sunday as usual, but even the grandchildren were subdued. Ben and Mary Alice came for lunch too. When they were seated round the table and having coffee, Mike raised the subject of the future of the ranch.

"Have you decided what you want to do, Mom?" he asked.

"No, not exactly. I know I want to stay here, but beyond that I just don't know."

"Can you handle this set-up on your own? We can all help out, but will you feel easier with a manager?"

"I don't know. I haven't given it much thought."

"That won't be necessary."

The voice was quiet, but she spoke with conviction. They all looked towards Rhona. She looked round the table and her eyes rested on her mother and she smiled at her.

"It has all been decided some time ago. Dad has taught me all I need to know. I can carry on from here. You see we talked over all of this. He told me what I must do if ever anything ever happened to him. It is strange. You'd have thought he could foresee the future."

Charlotte looked at her daughter. She was just seventeen, but in the past few days she had quite suddenly gained a maturity and composure.

"You are still at high school, Rhona," Charlotte remarked.

"That finishes in three weeks. I have completed all the exams. I needn't go back."

"And can you handle the ranch? Won't that be a problem?"

"No, Mom. I've handled the ranch before. There will be no problem."

Charlotte leaned back and closed her eyes. Of whom did her daughter remind her? Briefly she was transported to an old fort atop a Scottish hill. She felt the sun warm on her body and the strong arms round her as she listened to the story of Appin Mary. She could not have been any older than Rhona; and then Tom's voice came back to her.

"Rhona will have to do what Rhona has to do," it said.

Charlotte smiled wistfully to herself.

"Yes, that is how it will be," she thought. She opened her eyes

"You are sure, Rhona?"

"I'm sure."

"Then that is how it will be."

Rhona came round and kissed her on the cheek.

"Thanks, Mom. I think you will find that we are partners anyway. You see Dad left me his half-share of the ranch."

Charlotte clasped Rhona's hand to her cheek.

"Howdy, partner," she whispered.

Chapter Twenty-Two

Ben was waiting for her when she got back. The sun was already getting hot. He rose to greet her when she came up from the barn.

"Ben looks more biblical every time I see him," she thought. "He looks as though he has just stepped straight out of the Old Testament."

Ben had put on quite some weight over the years she had known him. He had a flowing iron-gray beard and his hair was almost white. Charlotte loved him dearly. Since Tom had died she turned to him more and more for advice. She came forward and kissed his cheek.

"Ben, it is lovely to see you. To what do I owe this pleasure?"

"You are a charmer, Charlotte. You always were and it is great to see you, too."

"Then come and have coffee."

She waited till Ben was ready to talk. Ben always took his time. Mostly he skirted round the main reason for his visit and talked of other matters first.

"I had a visit from Rhona and Angus yesterday. Now there's a magnificent young man. Angus is big and handsome and my boys are just full of admiration for him. They had heard all about him from Andrew Leslie and they were just longing for him to visit. They got to discussing the Highland Games right as soon as he arrived and he gave then a demonstration on throwing the hammer. They had a try and couldn't reach much more than halfway. Even Mary Alice was bowled over. She hugged and kissed him as soon as he arrived and I've never known her to do anything like that before. She was all starry-eyed over him and she is over sixty."

"Come, Ben, you exaggerate."

"I swear I don't, and he and Rhona make the most handsome couple I ever did see, and that's no exaggeration."

"They are. I've thought so myself, but let's not get round to matchmaking. That would be too complicated by far."

"If that's the way they are headed, the complications won't matter a dime."

"I think not. They are much more like just good friends. They tease each other all the time. I have never seen so much banter and teasing."

"Ah, well, it is all in good fun. They laugh a lot with it. Often that's just a prelude to courtship."

"Ben, I declare you are the most conniving man I ever did see. I think you are out of your depth in this case. I rather think Rhona is not too sure of herself, but I can't see romance with Angus being on the cards right now."

She paused.

"Do I really mean that, or is it just wishful thinking on my part?" she thought.

"Maybe. Maybe not. Angus is a swell guy. He is full of fun, but dependable with it.

However that was not what I came to talk with you about. You know that the Mayor of San Miguel is retiring in six months?"

This was the Ben she knew. Now he was getting down to the real reason for his visit. Ben had been born and brought up around San Miguel. He had seen it grow from a small hamlet to a sizeable town. He cared deeply for the town and for the whole county. He had doubtless decided on the person he wanted for Mayor.

"He wants my support and he'll get my wholehearted support. Ben does not make a choice like that lightly. It will be the right choice," she thought.

Ben lit his pipe and sat back in his chair.

"We want you to run for Mayor, Charlotte," he said.

It took a little time for the words to sink in.

"Ben, have you taken leave of your senses?"

"No, I have not. A group of us have given it a lot of thought. We are all agreed. You are the only choice."

"Ben, if you thought of it at all you would see that it isn't possible."

"Why not?"

"Oh, for a whole lot of reasons. I couldn't handle a job like that, for starters."

"Not so. You are Chairman of the Board of Governors for the High School. That is a highly responsible job. We all know you will handle that very well. Listen, Charlotte, you and Tom have made a great contribution to this county in the last twenty years, you even more than Tom. The Annual Rodeo would have died a natural death if it weren't for the efforts you put into reviving it. It is now the most important event for miles around. We know just what you are capable of."

Charlotte could not deny this. Every word he said was true.

"But, Ben, there are all kinds of personal reasons. Rhona is just nineteen. She is a very efficient and capable girl and she can handle this set-up on her own, but I don't want her to feel tied to the ranch for all time. She may feel she wants a break sometime. I would like her to have that break for however long it takes. I want to be here to take up the reins then, and besides I would miss the open spaces far too much. I would die without my ride out over the prairie."

"Charlotte, you can do the job of Mayor and have your ride over the range. All I am saying is think it over. Just think forward a little. You will see it makes sense."

Ben rose and crammed his battered old Stetson on top of his white locks.

"And, anyway," he murmured, "a woman like you could handle the ranch and the job of Mayor with no trouble."

Charlotte sat and pondered for a long time.

"Angus has made quite an impression on everyone," she thought. "Even Mary Alice. He has that same magnetism. Old as I am, I can still feel it. I wonder if Rhona will ever get around to experiencing the magnetism, and will she respond to it the way I did once? He is something quite out of the ordinary. Oh Tom, what a pity. He could so easily have been the some one special?"

"Are you going somewhere?" asked young Tom when Rhona came out to the patio.

"No. We are having dinner right here. Why do you ask?"

"Oh, no particular reason. It is just that we never see you wear a dress at home."

"Well, you are seldom at home, and, anyway, I'll thank you not to be so pass remarkable, young man."

"Ooh," Tom grimaced.

Charlotte looked at her daughter again and then again. She was a picture in her low-cut midnight blue dress with her hair swept to one side and falling over her left shoulder.

"My God! She is beautiful. She is radiant. I always thought she was a lovely girl, but this is real beauty," she thought.

"Will you have a bourbon, Angus?" asked Charlotte.

"Yes. Thanks."

"And you, Rhona?"

"I think I'll have a sherry," she said nonchalantly.

"And I think I shall have a fit if there are any more major surprises tonight," thought Charlotte, as she went to get the drinks. "I have been trying my best for months now to persuade Rhona to wear something other than jeans, and I have been tactfully suggesting that there are other drinks besides diet coke, without any success whatsoever, and suddenly in one night it all comes together. I wonder. I wonder."

Rhona was silent as she ate. She always had had a healthy appetite. She spent huge amounts of energy in her everyday activities. She never needed to think of diet. She burned up more calories than almost any one Charlotte knew. Tonight the blue eyes were dark with uncertainty. She picked at her food. Charlotte longed to put her arms round her daughter, but she didn't dare.

"I think I know what ails her," thought Charlotte. "Oh, why did they have to be of the same blood? What a tangled web life is."

Charlotte realised she was staring into her empty coffee cup.

"Time to put away your psychiatrist's couch," she advised herself. "Good Lord, life is difficult in many ways. I wonder how we hang on to our sanity."

They were all gathered on the verandah. Kelly and Young Tom were seated on cushions close to Angus.

"We are going to hog Angus all to ourselves," said Kelly. "You two have had him all to yourselves ever since he arrived."

"Yes, and they have been teaching me all about ranching in Texas. They have been great teachers, too, and Rhona has been telling me all manner of fascinating lore and stories."

"Well, maybe it is time you told us a few stories of the Highlands. Mom tells us the odd one now and again. I would love to go there and I shall one day, but, in the meantime, how about a tale or two?"

"I wouldn't want to bore you."

"No chance."

"Well, on condition that you will tell me if they become boring."

"Okay."

They sat enthralled as he unfolded some of the more spectacular tales of his native land.

Kelly had stars in her eyes. Charlotte's youngest daughter was showing an academic bent, something with which Charlotte was very happy. Angus told them of the story of Dairmid and the wild boar on Beinn an Tuirc.

"That is great stuff. I love stories of giants."

"Well, Dairmid wasn't really a giant, just a warrior. The real giants of Celtic lore are Finn McCool and Bennendonner."

"Who were?"

"Well, they were just a pair of giants."

"You are not getting off that lightly, Angus Maclean. You've mentioned them and now you just have to tell us the story."

"Are you sure?"

"Positive."

"All right, I'll trade you the story of the Giant's Causeway for a story of a Texas giant."

"Oh, well. Okay. I guess."

"Right, here goes."

"The Giant's Causeway is a world heritage geological site on the north -east coast of Ireland in County Antrim. These are volcanic rock formations pushed up in crystalline forms. There is a similar, if smaller, site on the Scottish island of Staffa. The site gets its name from two giants of Celtic mythology. The giants were called Finn McCoul, an Irish giant, and Bennendonner, a Scottish giant.

"The story goes that Finn McCoul, who lived in Ulster, had a habit of taunting Bennendonner. In fact, Finn McCoul was responsible for creating Lough Neagh in the middle of Ulster by picking up a clod of earth and throwing it at Bennendonner across what is now the North Channel between the Mull of Kintyre and County Antrim in Ulster. However, his aim was not very good and it fell into the sea and became the Isle of Man halfway between Ireland and England.

"Now, Bennendonner, the Scottish giant, got a teeny bit peeved by all this taunting and decided to go over to Ireland and sort out Finn McCoul once and for all, and so he built a causeway between Staffa and Antrim, and marched over to Ulster. Bennendonner was much bigger than Finn McCoul and when Finn saw just how big Bennedonner was he was sore afraid, as the good book says, and he ran and hid himself. But, you know, it isn't easy for a giant to hide himself and it would only be a matter of time before Bennendonner found him, and so it fell to Finn's wife to come up with a plan to save him.

"She dressed Finn up as a baby, and when Bennendonner saw the baby he said - if this is the size of the bairn, I have no desire to meet the father, and so he marched back to Scotland, destroying the causeway behind him, and all that can be seen of it now are those two rock formations at either end in County Antrim in Northern Ireland and on the Isle of Staffa at Fingal's Cave."

"Your turn now, Kelly."

"You know we are a mite short of giant stories in Texas. I guess the nearest we come is Pecos Bill."

"Right, tell me of Pecos Bill," said Angus.

"He's not quite in the same league as your giants."

"If he's anything like the rest of Texas, he'll match up any day."

"Oh, very well," said Kelly.

"Pecos Bill is said to have been born in Texas in the Eighteen thirties. According to lore, as an infant he used a bowie knife as a teething ring and played with bears and other wild animals. After falling out of his parents' wagon near the Pecos River in Texas, he became lost and was subsequently raised by coyotes. As an adult, he rode a mountain lion and used a rattlesnake as a whip. Later, he rode a horse named Widow-Maker, which no one else could ride, not even Bill's bride, Slue-Foot Sue, whom he met when she rode down the Río Grande on a catfish as large as a whale. During a dry year, Pecos Bill drained the Río Grande to water his ranch, which included the entire state of New Mexico."

"I'm afraid that not much more is known of Pecos Bill," said Kelly.

"Ah, Widow Maker and Slue-Foot Sue and a ranch which includes all of New Mexico. That certainly measures up. That's great stuff!" said Angus. "That is certainly game all."

Kelly was keen to follow a career in journalism. She had applied to all of the leading women's colleges in the Eastern States. She secretly hoped to go to Vassar. Its tradition of writers was the great attraction. Kelly was working hard to get top grades. Charlotte was sure she would get them, too. There was a quiet determination under the sunny exterior. Young Tom had set his sights on Harvard Business School. His father's early business leanings were coming out in his youngest son and so was his love of ranching. "He is so like his father," thought Charlotte. "He will make room in his life for both."

They were boarders in the High School, as were many of the ranching children. Charlotte dropped then at school on Monday mornings and collected them again on Friday afternoons. The system was tried and tested. It worked very well. Although Charlotte was Chairman of the Board of Governors of the school, she insisted that no special favours should come the way of her children.

Kelly was hanging on to every word Angus spoke and Rhona had asked Angus to repeat the story of Alan nan Sop.

"You are so lucky to have all that history. That is the stuff of great writing," said Kelly. "How I'd love to have such a family history to write about."

"Please feel free to write about mine," laughed Angus.

"Thanks, I might just do that one day; but seriously, the story-telling in families is something of great value. You can trace all sorts of things."

"Yes, I know what you mean. Take my father, for example. He has dark auburn hair and hazel eyes. He is the only one to have such colouring. We would be at a loss to explain that, if it were not for the fact we do know our family history. His colouring is a throwback of several generations and because we have been told about it in our younger days, sitting round the peat fire at night, we know just where it comes from."

"It isn't the same as yours, then?"

"No. I have the Maclean colouring. The Macleans have black hair and blue eyes. My father's colouring is a throwback to my great-great grandmother. She had auburn hair and hazel eyes. He is the only one of us who ever inherited her colouring. My great-great grandmother's people came over from France with Bonnie Prince Charlie. She was a romantic lady, was my Great-Great Grandmama."

"It sounds fascinating. Tell us about her," said Rhona.

"Oh, you might find it boring."

"I'm sure we shan't."

"Well, do stop me if you find it boring."

Like so many of the Celtic race, he was a born storyteller. He talked with his eyes, his hands and his body. His voice was soft and deep and it caressed the senses. Charlotte leaned back in the chair. She was thankful that she sat in the shadow. She closed her eyes and drifted gently back in time. The battlements of the old fort on top of the hill were crystal clear in her mind. She could see the standing stone and the kilt spread on the short grass and she again felt the tender strong arms round her, as the story of Appin Mary unfolded, and the sun warmed their nakedness. She had not forgotten one word of the story.

"Was that where Rhona had been conceived?" she wondered idly.

"So, that is the story of my Great- Great Grandmama," he concluded.

Charlotte looked at Rhona. She was staring at Angus, quite enraptured.

"Yes. Quite a lady," she said.

Charlotte longed to ask about Hector. Quite suddenly she longed to know what had happened to him. She wanted to know how he had survived the death of Bessie, but she could not trust herself to ask.

"Is your father a farmer too?"

Charlotte silently blessed her daughter for asking.

"No, said Angus. "He is an adventurer is Hector. That is my father's name. Red Hector, they call him in Gaelic. He had a tragic life when he was young. Perhaps I shouldn't tell you this, but then it won't mean anything to you anyway."

"Little do you know, dear Angus," thought Charlotte fondly.

"You see, Hector never did marry my mother. They played together as children and it developed into a romance and soon they became lovers. Hector was just sixteen when I was born. As was the custom, they were separated. Bessie - that was my mother's name - was sent to Edinburgh to have her child. That was I. Hector was sent to Glasgow to finish his studies. They were not supposed to have any contact, but they did. My grandparents brought me up. I only learned that Hector was my father on his wedding day."

"But that's barbaric. Why did they have to be separated?"

"I don't quite know. It has to do with our customs. That is the way they did things in those days. I know it is only twenty years ago, but habits and customs die hard in the Highlands."

"Hector and Bessie continued with their studies. They kept in touch with each other through a mutual friend. Hector took part in the Braemar Games for the first time that year. They arranged to meet in Perth after the games. On her way to meet Hector, Bessie was involved in a car accident near Perth. It was Hector who came across her car upended in the ditch. She would have died there and then if it hadn't been for him. It required superhuman strength to get the car out of the ditch. No one could ever work out how he managed it, but he did. He practically tore the car to pieces with his bare hand to get her out. They took her to hospital and Hector sat by her bedside for two days. She was conscious and I think supremely happy for much of that time, but then she suffered a brain hemorrhage and died."

Charlotte felt an ache at her heart and the tears welled up in her eyes. Her heart ached for Hector. She remembered how he had longed for Bessie. She relived, momentarily, the anguish she had experienced on the Q.E.2 when Tom had told her. Slowly she compassed herself.

"What a tragic story. How did your father get over it, Angus?" said Rhona.

"Oh, he was devastated, but he handled it well. He continued to compete in the Highland Games. He was always very bright academically. He threw himself into his studies and ended up with a Masters in Agriculture and a degree in Management Studies. He joined a Multinational and went to work abroad. A few years later he married a girl from Nether Lorne. Even then he had not yet had his fill of tragedy. This girl too was involved in an accident, but on a horse. She lost the child she was carrying and could never have any more. She was a fine woman. I was very fond of her. She mollycoddled me something terrible."

Angus took another sip of his drink and then he continued.

"They were very happy."

"Were?" said Charlotte in a strangled voice.

"Yes. Even then, there was yet more tragedy in store for him. She died in his arms. She too suffered a brain hemorrhage, the result of her fall many years before. Poor Hector, I have never seen anything like it. He was a totally broken man. He gave up his job and lived with my grandparents in the village and he worked himself almost to death round the farm just so he could fall into the oblivion of sleep at night. For months he moved around like the living dead. I hope I never have to live through anything like that again in my life."

"Did he get over it?" asked Rhona with concern.

"Yes, he is nothing if not a fighter is Hector. In time he did get over the trauma sufficiently to pick up the threads of life. I think my two sons did more to get him on his feet than anything else."

Hector

The jet climbed steadily through the clouds, which hung in the azure sky above Lagos like great lumps of the softest cotton wool. Now and then there was just the slightest hiccup in the smooth flight of the plane as it entered another bank of cloud and then quite suddenly it rose clear of the cloud layer and carried on in its smooth flight path. The clouds were well broken just now, but they were becoming thicker by the day and soon Nigeria would sigh with relief as another rain season delivered it from the months of drought.

Quite soon the seatbelt was switched off and they were approaching the dun-coloured desert. Hector's brow creased with concern as he thought of the call he had had from Angus the night before last. He had never called before when he was abroad. He must have been really concerned about Jane. It had taken just a day for Hector to hand over to his number two and catch a plane for home. He had few concerns about handing over. Sally Onduku could handle the company just as well as he could.. She was the most capable of all the executives in Nigeria.

Now they were over the Sahara and an endless vista of sand dunes. He took a drink from the stewardess and sat back to take stock. He had come a long way in the last few years. He was never quite sure of the exact reason for his meteoric rise up the ladder of his organisation. Certainly, he was blessed with a fine intellect as well as physical attributes. He was immensely popular in the community and his work was well received and commented on throughout the organisation, but he had a faint suspicion that some aspects of his private life also played a part.

Life for him had become a succession of exotic locations starting with Bombay and then Honduras and most recently Lagos. He smiled as he thought of the hell-raising days there with his American friend Chuck. They had become legends in the bars and pleasure houses of Tegussi Galpa. The charmed life style was punctuated by equally anticipated periods of peace and quiet when he returned to Nether Lorne on leave every year. He always enjoyed coming home. He stayed with his parents and met old friends and of course there was Angus - above all there was Angus.

His chest swelled with pride as Angus grew in size and character. He loved Angus beyond everything else on earth and Angus followed him everywhere. He idolised this big brother who, every year, came home with stirring stories of his life abroad. Hector sometimes wondered if Angus would follow in his footsteps, but there was little indication that he would. The farm was his life from a very early age and he longed only for the day when he would have his own farm.

Hector smiled to himself when he thought of that year when Angus was thirteen. He was at home that year for his twenty-ninth birthday and that was when he met Jane Hunter at a dance. She was some four years younger than he. She was tall and willowy and by reputation willful and stubborn. A few men had courted her briefly but had given up.

"How is the most eligible bachelor this evening?" she asked.

"Who, me?" he said.

"None other," she said. "The catch of the moment."

"Then why don't you try to catch me?" he asked.

"I have a better idea. Why don't you try to catch me?"

"I think I might just do that," he said.

He liked the spirit of this blond girl and he wooed her constantly. They were married six weeks later. His elder brother stood in as his best man and Angus was the chief usher. He was proud in his first long trouser suit.

On his wedding morning Angus had come into his room. He sat fidgeting on the edge of the bed.

"Is something bothering you?" asked Hector.

"'Not bothering me exactly."

"Then what?"

"Mother and father have been talking to me," he said.

"Oh yes, and what about?"

Angus was hesitant.

"Well, they told me that you are really my father and that they are in fact my Grandparents."

Hector was taken aback. The subject had not been discussed.

"Yes, that is quite correct. I had not realised they were going to tell you. Does it upset you?"

"No. Not at all. In fact I am very pleased about it. I have been thinking it over since last night and if you don't mind I shall still call them Mother and Father. I have got used to it and I shall continue to *call you Hector in public, but to myself I shall always call you Daddy - if you don't mind?"*

He put his arm round the boy's shoulder. Tears welled in his eyes.

"That will make me very happy and very proud. I am more proud of that than anything that has ever happened to me."

Angus threw his arms round his neck.

"Okay, Daddy," and then, embarrassed at showing his feelings, he quickly moved to the subject of his duties for the day. He was maturing fast and getting big. With a shock of black hair and intense blue eyes, he was in the tradition of Maclean men.

"I hope he has an easier adolescence than I had," thought Hector. "I shall have to see that he knows what is in store for him and is better prepared than I was."

"Yes, you are growing up, Angus. When I come back from my honeymoon we must have a talk. There are some things you should know about and also what is in store for you."

"I would like that," said Angus, "There are so many things I am just beginning to think about."

"We shall have to think about what you are going to do when you are older too."

"Oh, I know what I am going to do," said Angus. "I am going to be a farmer. I've never wanted to be anything else and, talking of that, I had better go and feed the calves."

Hector mused as he had his bath and shaved. It seemed strange that he was only twenty-nine but he had a thirteen-year-old son - a son of whom any man would be proud.

After the honeymoon they returned to the house they had bought in the village. It was a delightful old house by the river. They spent the remainder of his leave there and Angus was a constant visitor. Jane was only ten years older than Angus. They were the greatest of friends from the start.

The marriage was idyllic apart from one great sadness. She fell pregnant on her honeymoon and, four months later, Jane miscarried after falling from a horse. She was also badly concussed. When she recovered, the doctors told her she would never bear a child. She and Hector were desolate for some time, but she gradually became philosophical.

"It could be worse," said Jane. "At least, we have a son already and I couldn't love anyone more than I do him."

Their marriage was never anything other than a wondrous experience for both of them. True, there were a few ups and downs. Jane developed headaches. It was nothing serious, but there was a dull and constant ache, for which they could find no explanation. She became an accomplished hostess and was a great asset in every community in which she mingled. The highlights of her life, though, were at home in Scotland. Hector recalled the thrill she felt when Angus got married. He got married just after his eighteenth birthday and a year later became the father of robust son. Hector was never quite sure whether it was her health, or the attraction of the new grandchild, which caused Jane to stay back when he returned to Nigeria after his annual leave. She poured out all the affection on the child which she would have given to the son she herself never had. Hector reluctantly left without her. She promised him she would join him after a month or two.

She was much more of a friend to Angus and her new daughter-in-law than a stepparent. Morag was young and more than pleased to have help. Angus continued to adore his new *mother. He had never felt at ease calling her 'Mother', but was delighted to have the chance to call her 'Grandma'.*

Hector thought of the phone call he had had the night before. It was from Angus. Angus had never called him at work before, but he said he was becoming increasingly worried about Jane.

"Nothing serious at present," he had said, "but I think you should come back soon."

Hector returned home four days before his thirty-eighth birthday. The reason he gave Jane was that he had been recalled to head office and had persuaded them to give him some leave. She was delighted to have him home. He talked to her doctor who could give him little information.

"It will require a brain scan," the doctor said. "The neurologists can find nothing wrong, but there is something amiss. Until we can get a scan arranged, then she should just continue as normal."

On the night of his thirty-eighth birthday they had a quiet dinner at home. The grandchildren had gone home and they were alone. After dinner, Jane said, "Do you remember the night before we were married we went for a walk up the hill to the cairn? I should love to go there again."

"You mean tonight? Why not? It is a lovely night."
They walked slowly up the glen in the quiet of the evening. It was still warm. The evening chill had not yet set in. They sat by the cairn. Below them the woods were dark-green. The westering sun bathed the sea in rose pink and the doves cooed softly. They were happy. They were content. He gently stroked her hair and then he drew her down beside him. Their love was slow and tender and then they walked slowly back down the hill.

When they reached home she brought him a whisky and sat down on his knee. She put her arms round his neck and snuggled down into him.

"Happy birthday, my Darling," she whispered. *"You know I love you to distraction. I have had ten of the happiest years of my life since I married you. No matter what happens, no one can ever take that away from me. I do love you so."*

"And I love you too. I can't begin to tell you how much. I have never been so happy and content."

"That is the nicest thing you could possibly say to me."

She laid her head on his chest and stroked his hand. She sighed softly.

He stroked her hair gently. Through the open door dusk was falling. In the garden a thrush was beating a snail against a stone. The only sounds were the murmur of the stream and the birdsong. Peace and contentment lay all around.

It was quite some time before he realised that she had died in his arms.

The crystal water splashed between the stones and at the edges of the stream the ice formed exquisite patterns. The sun shone from a clear blue sky and the frost was sparkling diamonds in the fields. A tiny wren flitted among the dark branches of the hazel trees. The beauty of winter had always delighted Hector. He had always loved the countryside in all of the seasons, but winter, for him, had its own special charms. Now he looked at this magical scene without interest. His eyes took in the patterns of colour and light and shade, but they no longer meant anything to him. No emotions stirred within him.

That is how things were with him these days. Nothing aroused any feelings in him. He was an empty shell. He went about his daily toil *like some empty mechanical being which wore itself out with physical effort during the day so that it could fall into the blessed oblivion of sleep at night. The sleep at least relieved him for a while of the dreadful emptiness and the pain of guilt and remorse which was with him all of his waking hours.*

They had tried to help him. They were there with him every day and slowly they despaired of reaching him and they began to leave him to himself and they prayed and prayed that he would find peace.

But there were two who would not leave him be. There were two sturdy little boys who did not understand his grief and his need to be on his own. They could only remember the Grandpa who had filled their lives with so much fun only a few short months ago. They wanted him back and were relentless in their quest. They climbed upon his knee and they clambered over him and they hugged and kissed him and they pierced the armour he had built around himself and they let chinks of light into his soul and they began to melt the ice, which surrounded his heart.

Chapter Twenty-Three

"Did I hear right? Did he say his sons?" thought Charlotte. She looked towards Rhona and she knew that she had heard correctly. Rhona looked down towards the floor. Her face was a mask.

"He went visiting friends in Honduras," continued Angus, quite oblivious to the devastation his last remark had caused.

"Sam, his friend, was also a psychologist and therapist. He cured Hector very quickly. It was something of a miracle. Hector bounced back and he is now heavily involved in one of the old wine houses in London of all things and he has a new girlfriend. I am very relieved. She is the Honourable Sarah Noble, from a family of English landed gentry. I believe there is a child on the way. I think they will be married soon. They seem very happy. You know, I hope it is a little girl. I've always wanted a little sister."

"And you've had a little sister for nineteen years," thought Charlotte to herself.

Charlotte sighed a sigh of relief. She found it strangely comforting that Hector had found happiness at last.

"Why does it affect me so after all of those years?" she wondered inwardly.

"I suppose it is the knowledge that we have something in common."

She looked towards her daughter. Rhona still looked downward. Her face was a study of bewilderment. She was shaking her head slightly as she tried to come to terms with the reality of what she had just heard and then she sat up straight.

"Did I hear you say something about your two sons?" said Rhona.

Charlotte looked at her again. She had regained much of her composure. "She too is a survivor," thought Charlotte. "Just like her father."

"Oh yes, those two rascals. You know, I miss them."

"You are married then?"

"Oh, yes, I'm married. Of course I am; but you knew that, didn't you?"

Rhona shook her head.

"I never thought of mentioning it. I thought you were aware of it. That just goes to show how completely absorbing this trip has been. Mind you, we've talked of nothing else but ranching. All that and this wonderful country and I just never got round to talking about my family. I haven't forgotten them. They are always the last thing I think of at night and the first thing I think of in the morning. I'm sorry about that. You see, we put all those personal details down on our fact sheets along with what we do."

"Sorry. That's my fault," said Rhona. "We've been just so busy. I never did get round to looking at the fact sheets. I intended doing that later tonight."

"You are young to have two sons, Angus," said Charlotte.

"I'm twenty-two past. We got married at eighteen. I think my grandparents were anxious to see that I did not quite go down the same road as my father. He was just sixteen when I was born.. We have three children now. Our daughter is just reaching the crawling stage. She is a sweetie."

"She's handling this very well," thought Charlotte. "I suspect she is devastated, but it doesn't show."

"So who's looking after the farm?"

"Morag, that's my wife, and my grandfather. He is still very active. This is a quiet time of year. They will manage very well for ten days. I was quite keen to make this trip when the opportunity arose. You see, there will be little chance of another for a few years and I did want to see a little bit of the world. I don't think I could have chosen a better part than Texas."

"That's sweet of you to say. Didn't your father ever want to be a farmer?" asked Rhona.

"No! Hector could never settle down to be a farmer. He has the world at his feet. He needs excitement and travel and the cut and thrust of business life. He is successful too. He was at one time the heavyweight champion of all the Highlands."

"Is that your ambition too? You impressed everyone over at Ben's the other night."

"No, Rhona. I'm not serious enough to be a champion. I do take part in the local Highland Games, but nothing more. I am too much of a Maclean. We tend to be boisterous and too fond of fun to be serious and you have to be serious to be a champion. Besides, it has fallen to my lot to keep up the family traditions. Mind you, I am very happy to do so. I hope at least one of my sons will be a farmer too."

Charlotte snuggled down again under the quilt. She went over in her mind the events of the evening. In a way the main problem had been solved, but there remained the mending of Rhona.

"She is more her father's daughter than you are your father's, son, Angus," she thought. "You described your father well and while you were doing so you could have been describing Rhona. I know that now. I suppose I have known that all along. I was just unable to admit to it. But, yes, I know now that she cannot be tied to the ranch for all time. She too will need the stimulus of travel and excitement. Yes she will always love the ranch and I suspect she will always return to it, but she will need more in her life than just the ranch. How we shall handle that problem I don't yet know. Thankfully, young Tom is keen on ranching and Mike and Ben are always there. Anyway, we shall manage. Now that I know, I can make plans."

Chapter Twenty-Four

Charlotte became aware of the smiles on the faces of Sue Ellen and Maria and she realised she was singing at the top of her voice. She sang quite often and with gusto, particularly when she had got over some difficulty in her life   She remembered the first time she had sung with such lack of restraint. She was, at the time, traveling along the banks of Loch Lomond and she was off on an adventure, which had changed her life.

"Oh, Tom," she whispered to herself, "I don't regret that journey. I was happy then. I am even happier today."

The big ranch kitchen was bustling as they prepared the food for the party that evening. The wives of the cattlemen had come to help her, and elsewhere in the county Mary Alice was similarly employed, as were Charlotte's three daughters-in-law. It was to be the biggest party ever held at Lone Pine Ranch. Charlotte was not quite sure how many people would attend, but she thought the number would be close to two hundred, and that would include the ten Scottish Young Farmers who would be leaving them tomorrow.

Usually, on rodeo night, they a small drinks party in town for those organising the rodeo, but Charlotte wanted to do something special this year.

"I think you are crazy, Charlotte. Half the county will want to attend," said Ben, when she told him and Mary Alice two nights before.

"Oh, Ben, it will mean a little extra work, I suppose, but I don't mind. I feel I have to do something to repay the wonderful hospitality I received all those years ago in Scotland."

"Well I can't see how you will manage to handle those preparations and open the Rodeo at the same time."

"Simple, Ben. I will get some one to open the Rodeo on my behalf and I can't think of anyone better than you."

"But you always open the Rodeo - you have done that for the last ten years."

"Well, it is time we had a change."

"I suspect you are hatching a plot, Charlotte. You have that air about you. Anyway, the rodeo won't be properly opened unless it is you who does it. So just set your mind to that fact. You will put in an appearance at the Rodeo, and you will open it. Won't you?"

"I am not hatching any plots, Ben, and, yes, of course I shall be at the Rodeo. I would not miss that for the world."

"And you will open it?"

"Oh Well, if you insist."

"I insist."

"Oh, all right then. I'll do it for this year again, but we must think in terms of a change for next year."

"I can't see the need, myself."

"Don't you pay him no heed," said Mary Alice. "You just go ahead. We shall all help you. Men don't understand those things."

The swirling dust, the smell of sweat from man and animal, the sensation of excitement, it was all there. Charlotte never ceased to feel the thrill of the rodeo. This was the most successful Rodeo ever. The visitors from Scotland threw themselves into the proceedings. They took part in many of the events at the cost of only a few bruises and aching muscles. Only Angus took no active part. He was the only one in his kilt.

"I am not about to give away any secrets concerning our national dress by sitting on a bucking bronco in a kilt," he laughed.

He did, however, draw the biggest cheer of the day. That came at the end of the day when he drew the tickets for the prize draw. When he announced that Amy McIvor had won first prize in the draw, Angus strained his huge muscles, lifted the beribboned steer off the ground and carried it over to her.

Things had worked out well. It had taken a big decision to go to Rhona's room last night. Rhona was sitting up in bed and Charlotte had gone in and sat beside her.

"We've never really indulged before in girlie talk, Rhona," she began.

"And I guess you think the time has come," said Rhona.

"Maybe. Were you keen on him?"

"I fell in love with him, Mom. I fell head over heels. He seemed friendly enough putting his arm round my shoulders and lifting me down from the horse. Maybe I was just too much of an innocent. I think maybe I just read too much into his friendly gestures. Oh, God, I just don't know."

"That is just the way of the Highlanders, Rhona. In many ways it is they who are the innocents. I love them dearly. They are so straightforward and open. If he put his arm round you, or if he gave you a peck on the cheek, then it is just because he liked you a lot. They are affectionate, open, lovely, simple people. They are much more open about expressing simple affection than we are. I can see any one misunderstanding them. I suppose you have to live with them for a while to really appreciate and understand them. No, Rhona, he didn't lead you on."

"Oh, God, Mom, I have been a fool. How could I have been so foolish?"

"You weren't foolish. What happened was perfectly natural. Who wouldn't fall for a big strong handsome man like him? The truth to tell, I was just a little in love with him myself and Ben tells me Mary Alice got all starry-eyed over him."

"Gee, Mom, I'm real glad you told me that. I think he is a swell guy. You know I had such a lot of fun with him and he always treated me like an equal. I would hate to think he might have gone off and left the wrong impression. I really like the guy. I can't explain it. Quite apart from falling for him, I just kind of really like the guy. Mom, I'm going to need some time off tomorrow. I want to go buy some presents for his children."

When she got back to her room, Charlotte thought long and hard and then she picked up the phone and called Dallas.

"Charlotte, whatever is the matter?" said Connie. "You've never called me at this time of night. Is something seriously wrong?"

"No, Connie, nothing seriously wrong; perhaps a little delicate, but not seriously wrong."

"Intriguing, Charlotte - spill the beans."

"Well, Connie, as you know we have those visitors from Scotland with us just now."

"Don't I ever know it, Charlotte? I am just as sick as a parrot that I've got myself all tied up here with this charity bash and I couldn't take up your invite for the party tomorrow night."

"Yes, I'm so sorry you couldn't come. You would have loved it. The visitors are just a great bunch of guys. Our own visitor is a big happy contented handsome young man. We are just thrilled to have him."

"She didn't fall for him?"

"Yes, she did. She's not the only one. My own heart missed a beat or two and Ben says Mary Alice went all starry-eyed over him."

"Oh, shit, and I'm stuck here in Dallas!"

"Connie, I've never heard you use a word like that before!"

"Well, I'm using it now and I feel a heap better for having used it, but carry on."

"Oh, Connie, life is so complicated these days. Nothing seems straightforward any more. Angus is married. Not only that but he has three children."

"Why, Charlotte, I'm just so surprised at Rhona going for a married man."

"That's the problem. She didn't know he was married. Not that he tried to hide it in any way; it was all there in the briefing notes. He assumed we knew. Rhona just hadn't got round to reading the notes."

"But didn't he mention his family?"

"Connie it was just one of those things. They were all tied up in ranching and things Texan. They are very much alike in many ways. You know how competent Rhona can be and the quiet determination she brings to things? Well, Angus matches her all the way. They got on like a house on fire. I've never seen two people get on so well. They made a lovely couple. They lived, ate and slept things Texan and Scottish Highlands. He was very keen to learn about ranching and horses and she was delighted to have the chance to teach him. So much so, that he just never got round to talking much about his family. They talked of nothing else but horses and ranching."

"Did you know she was falling for him?"

"I was pretty sure she had fallen for him. She started acting out of character and the night the kids came home from school, she appeared in a formal dress. She looked beautiful, Connie, and she had a sherry instead of a Coke."

"Lordy, Charlotte, you have been hoping for that for a long time."

"Yes, and it happened all of its own accord. That and a few other signs made me pretty sure."

"How did she find out?"

"That was Kelly's doing. She wanted to hog Angus all to herself when she came back from school. You know what a girl she is for listening to stories. Well, Angus was like a gold mine for her. Like many Highlanders he is a born storyteller. They were trading legends and talking about family histories and when Angus was talking about his father he just casually mentioned it. His father, Hector, has had a spectacular life. It was also quite tragic at times. Angus was telling Kelly of how his father was a broken man after the death of his wife.

He mentioned casually that his, Angus's, two sons did more to get Hector back to normality than anyone. You know, Connie, I was just so proud of her. I knew from the look on her face that she was devastated, but she is a survivor. She tackled the situation head-on. It was then that the information in the fact sheet came to be known."

"Oh the poor darling."

"Yes, but she rose above it all. I think, though, that she needs a break. I wondered if you could engineer a reason for her to come to Dallas?"

"I don't have to look too far for that, Charlotte. There are one or two here who are trying to unseat me. You know organisation has never been my strong point and I could sure use Rhona's help right about now. She's really great on that. Yes I sure could use her help."

"Fine, Connie - I'll tell her. You won't mention the romance."

"Charlotte, I'll be the soul of discretion."

"You seem to be getting well entrenched in your role as Queen Bee of Dallas society," said Charlotte.

"You bet your sweet life I am," said Connie. "You know, Charlotte, I used to envy you your position of Queen Bee of Beaumont society and then when you and Tom gave it all up I just seemed to inherit that from you. You see, when Bob died he left me so much goddamn money and when we moved to Dallas, taking over as Queen Bee seemed the natural thing to do then, and I just seem to have carried on from there. There are one or two in this town who would love to take over, as I said, and they will one day, but not yet, not till I am good and well ready."

"Well spoken. That's my girl."

"Yes, well, it is something of a game. I am quite content to play the game just now, but it isn't a great big deal. What are important to me now are my godchildren, Rhona and the three of your grandchildren. I was thrilled to bits being asked to be Rhona's godmother. And then when Mike asked me to be Godmother to his second, I was just over the moon, and then the other two boys followed suit and I was just ecstatic. How thrilled my Bob would be if he knew that Gary's boy was named after him. Charlotte, I'll never stop being just so grateful that I am so deeply involved with you and your family. It means just everything to me."

"I am delighted to hear that, Connie, and thanks. You know we all love you dearly. Neither Tom nor myself have any surviving sisters, so you are their only aunt. It means a lot to us all."

Charlotte could hear the sounds of indrawn breath.

"The hell with my eye makeup. This is happy crying," Connie sniffed.

Rhona was especially caring towards Angus next morning. Over breakfast she fussed over him and asked him all about his children and his wife, Morag. It began as friendly interest but she soon became absorbed in his description of the Highland way of life and of his own family. If he was in any way aware of the havoc he had unwittingly caused her, he did not show it. It was she who insisted he wear his kilt to the Rodeo.

When they came back from the rodeo she suggested he call Morag.

"But it will cost the earth," he protested.

"Think nothing of it. I think we can stand it," she laughed.

They left him in the privacy of the living room to make his call. After a little he came to call Rhona to the phone.

"Morag says she would like very much to talk to you, Rhona. Now don't let her keep you on the phone too long."

She was gone for quite some time and Angus kept drawing Charlotte's attention to the time.

"Relax, Angus," she said. "It isn't every day you know."

Rhona emerged from the living room just then.

"Morag wants to talk with you for a moment, Angus, but don't be too long and don't hang up whatever you do. We are nowhere near finished talking yet."

He shrugged his shoulders in resignation.

"They've been talking for an hour now," said Angus. "Would you like to maybe tell them?"

"No, Angus, and neither should you. I don't think either of us would be thanked real warmly for interrupting them right now."

Charlotte had a moment's concern when Rhona emerged dabbing her eyes with a tissue.

"Oh, Mom, they are just the sweetest guys. Morag is just the sweetest person. She has invited me over there this summer. I have to go for the christening of their daughter. Mom, they are going to call her Rhona and they have asked me to be her godmother. Oh, Mom, I'm just so proud and happy and honoured."

"How very good of them. That really is something and I am just so happy for you. You will go, of course."

"Yes, Mom, I sure will. You see Morag has been making plans for us. I hope you have enjoyed your stay here, Angus."

"I certainly have. No doubt about that."

"And you feel good and rested?"

"Of course."

He raised his eyebrows and threw her a suspicious look.

Charlotte too raised her eyebrows.

"You see, Mom, Morag feels she too needs a break. She said she would love to show me around when I come over there, and we are kind of planning."

"Oh! Oh!" said Angus.

"Morag plans on having the christening some time late August. That would give us the chance to see the Edinburgh Festival and the Braemar Highland Games."

Charlotte felt a pang of nostalgia as the names slipped so innocently off Rhona's tongue.

"And who will look after the children?"

"Yes, I did ask that, and Morag says the grandparents live nearby and her own mother will help and then, of course, there is dear Angus. He's had his holiday. He'll be all refreshed and able."

"I knew it was a bad mistake to let them talk so long. A whole hour! Who knows what mischief women can get up to in that time?"

"Only an hour. Now there's restraint. Of course, we haven't finished talking and planning yet. I am going to call her next week to make sure they all got home safely. Morag says she will plan a bit more before then."

Angus held his head in his hands.

"I think I'll break the piggy bank and buy some shares in the telephone company," he groaned.

"She'll have a great time in Scotland and she's quite thrilled and honoured at the thought of being Godmother, and why shouldn't she?" thought Charlotte as she dressed for the party. "After all, she is the baby's aunt. I'm sure somewhere subconsciously there is a feeling of kinship at work there. I wonder what became of Hector? I find myself thinking of him more and more ever since I discovered that he is Rhona's natural father."

Hector

Jack mused as he waited for Hector. He remembered the first time they met. Every eye in Bombay airport followed Hector that morning and not a few with open desire in them. He remembered standing with Prem Bahl at a cocktail party soon after.

"I think almost every woman in this room would like to take Hector to her bed" he said, " and I shall be surprised if not a few of them do just that before many months have passed."

"Prem had read the situation very accurately," thought Jack. "He really is a very spectacular man and there is not a mean bone in his body. In spite of a lifestyle that is pure drama and adventure, he is innocent as a newborn lamb."

Jack Ashley looked after Hector's finances. They had spent many enjoyable hours together on the first tour of duty abroad, but Jack had left because he found the lifestyle too restricting. He had no stomach for the regimentation of the multinational. He had set himself up as an investment manager and Hector was his first client. Some of the other company personnel followed suit and very soon he had a thriving set-up in the city. Having won his freedom, he was not about to compromise it by following the city rules. He had unfashionably long hair and, while he did wear a sober suit, his floral waistcoats and his rotund person were not in the best traditions of the City. At weekends he donned denim and leather jacket and set off on his bike with the others of this vanishing breed. Their numbers included carpenters and councilors, draughtsmen and dropouts and even a vicar. The city regarded him with a degree of amusement and respect. His record on investment was second to none.

Hector was a non-smoker and he drank very moderately. His excesses were food and sex. He required very substantial quantities of both. He was a gourmet nevertheless.

"Welcome to the club Hector," said Jack, when he was seated.
"What club is that?"
"The millionaire' club."
"Seriously?"
"Seriously, and by quite a margin."
"Great work, Jack. Very well done and thanks a million. Well, I'm damned!"
"Well, you are welcome, and, in return for that intelligence, you can buy me lunch and I shall choose the most expensive items on the menu"
"Well, I can't say I can't afford it, can I? You are very welcome, Jack."
They ordered martini cocktail. It arrived ice-cold.
"You know what, friend Hector, you are getting a reputation in the city."
"Balls, Jack! No one in the city has ever heard of me."
"A lot of people in the city have heard of you. The city is the most gossipy place you will find in all of London. I find them fascinating from a psychologist's point of view."
Hector had forgotten that Jack had majored in psychology long before he thought of the city and finance.
"I wonder why my best friends are psychologists?" he thought idly. "Even Sadie, in her way, was something of a therapist."
"I think it is because they sit at desks or computers and totally inanimate objects, that they have romantic outlooks," continued Jack. "They admire the swashbuckling hero. There are not too many these days. You fill that bill."
"Jack, have you been drinking all morning?"
"Not a drop. I am right. I know I am. You did the unusual. A troubleshooter for one of the big setups and then you drop out of sight. You surface later and buy a controlling interest in a nightclub, which is on its uppers. You have the guts to go for a bunch of unknowns, not one of whom was even fully qualified. It worked. It got publicity that no one could have dreamed of. That was pure good fortune."
"There it was, a Sunday Supplement with a business page that no one in the city wants to read on a Sunday, but which no one can afford to miss. The result is that they read through the business part as fast as possible, and pass on to the next part as quickly as they can, and there is what they really want on Sunday. The

entertainments and Yuppie Society column, with its outrageous writer, Tommy Bullen. He is an excellent writer, by the way. He has never done a better one than the one he did on 'God Apollo'."

Hector was accustomed to Jack. There were times when he got into full flight. It was best not to interrupt him. Left to himself, he provided sophisticated entertainment of an unbelievable quality. This hippy biker in the city threads had an I.Q. which was out of sight. At times, in small groups, and with people he liked, his gifts of expression were wondrous. Today he was in a fine mood. Hector sat entranced while he sipped his second martini and through his first glass of champagne. During the unfolding of the account of the city gents on Sunday, there was, miraculously, a meal gourmet proportions ordered.

"Just imagine it," Jack continued, "the city gent who has been shuffling paper all week. Thoreau said the mass of men live lives of quiet desperation. In the city the desperation isn't even quiet. They read of a club on its uppers. Along comes a man of mythological proportions and rescues it. In the process he gives the chance of a lifetime to a group of young men. They repay him with some of the most exciting decor ever seen in London. The cuisine is not far behind. They base the decor on their Hero. It has to be classic Greek. The piece de resistance is the statue. My God, Tommy Bullen's account of that and the way it was created was superb. Do you know, it was reckoned that you were responsible for more wet dreams and more furtive wankings that weekend, than occurred for the rest of the year?"

"You are full of shit, Jack."

"Not my statistics, but I believe them."

"The city gents all envied you. I wonder why the Scots are so self-effacing?"

"We are not particularly."

"You are. There you are with a superb physique, and hung in heroic proportions. You should be advertising the fact."

"I didn't need to. The bloody statue did that for me."

Jack roared with laughter.

"I gather it is still there."

"Yes, I tried to get its removal as part of the sale, but it seems to be an emotive entity. It arouses the most extreme passions. I have to give in every time. I can't imagine what possessed me to allow them to use my naked body to make the mould for that statue."

"So that was how it was done?"

"Yes, they did it in sections using plaster and then put them together and filled it with some new plastic material."

"Most of us were convinced it was marble."

"Yes, it looks like marble. I just wish it was not so bloody realistic, particularly since Tommy Bullen decided to plaster it all over his tabloid."

"Well, anyway, the city gents saw you as a hero. You were doing what they all secretly wanted to do. Your size helped too. That experiment with the gang really took their fancy. The place is a howling success and then you go and sell out for a fantastic profit and make sure the interests of the gang are protected. You are regarded as lucky, too. That in the city means a lot. Yes, you are a hero."

"I wish some of the luck had brushed off on my friends in the House of Noble."

"My God, Hector, there was a farce! Why didn't you advise them?"

"'Well, I was not involved at that time. I was keeping out of things and for a good reason."

"The fair Sarah, no doubt."

"The fair Sarah. I was being kept up with what was going on, in retrospect. I did not get the chance to tell them the way do it was to go to professionals and let them deal with the city. They should have known it. What is the objection of the city? The House of Noble is not that bad."

"The one objection is the management – your friends, in other words. They have been a pair of playboys for years. No one believes they are about to change."

"I thought that would be it."

"Not only have they bungled the approach to the financing, they are looking in the wrong place for their premises and plant. That should be out of London. The proper place is about one hour from London. Labour in London is unreliable and costly. The difference one hour out and the better reliability much more than offsets the extra transport costs. Peterborough and such places that is where they want to look."

"Or Wiltshire," said Hector.

"Or Wiltshire, probably better. Anyway do tell me what you have been up to that prevented you from telling them?"

"I've been to France for a second holiday with Sarah. We had a superb holiday together, but she had to go home because of the crisis. We are to be married soon."

"That is the best news. You have done well, Maclean. She is a fine girl and very attractive too. When is the wedding?"

"Not yet decided, but it will be fairly soon. You see, there is one slight complication. We are to become parents."

" Even better. That is wonderful news. I'll buy you lunch. That deserves a special toast."

"A small one. I have to catch the two thirty to Wiltshire. Manny did get me on the phone and persuaded me to go with him. He was going to brief me on the drive down, but Sarah rang and told me she wanted to see me before that. There is something personal she wants to discuss before we get too tied up with the business side of the House of Noble. That is why I am going by train."

"I have brought several offers from the city - good ones. I meant to nail you down here to put them to you, but I shall delay them. That is the only reason I would have accepted for doing so. I wish you both every happiness"' he said, raising his glass. "By the way, why don't you suggest new management for the House of Noble?"

"It would be the answer, but that would be up to Sarah's father. It would be easier, if it were not for the family connection. What to do with Manny and Eric is the big problem. They are not bad guys. They have a lot going for them. They would be excellent in sales."

"You have hit it on the head - quite squarely on the head. The Honourable Emanuell and the Honourable Eric, they have all the right club and society connections. It couldn't be better. Add to that the fact that they are such excellent company and you can't lose. There are so many snobs around in business it isn't true. All the guys from humble backgrounds who have made it under their own steam, and who should be proud of their humble backgrounds, instead want to bury them. An Honourable will be like a gold bar to them, and add to that the underlying romantic tendencies of most Americans, and the respect of Europeans, and the trust in our Aristocracy of the Arabs, and you have a setup that can't be bettered. You have a plan for the House of Noble. Don't you?"

"What makes you think that?"

"I have been around you too long, Hector. I can read you like a book, just from your chance remarks."

"Nonsense, Jack."

"Nonsense nothing. I'll tell you pretty well what you have decided too."

"With your newfound wealth you are going to buy a sizeable share in the House of Noble. You are going to locate the business end in Wiltshire and the office and sales in London. If they have any sense they will make you their Chief Executive, and, without a doubt, within a year you will have turned round another dead in the water business into a roaring success. By the way what about the product, the wine?"

"You know, Jack Ashley, as recently as one hundred and fifty years ago they were burning people like you at the stake. I begin to think there was considerable justification for the practice."

"Then, I am correct in my assessment?"

"I am proposing to buy a twenty percent share for half a million. The storage and handling will be transferred to Wiltshire. There is a mothballed farm steading there, which they can convert very easily for that purpose on Sir Ivor's estate. He is Sarah's father, by the way."

Jack nodded.

"The sales and publicity will be handled in the premises in St. James's It is proposed that Manny and Eric take special courses to upgrade their skills to that end, as they say. There is to be an Extraordinary General Meeting of the shareholders tonight to put forward those proposals and, just to make your day, dear Jack, Sir Ivor is going to propose that I be appointed Chief Executive."

"Ah, touché."

"Of course, these are just ideas. Translating them into reality could be very difficult indeed."

"I know a big hairy Highlander who could do it," said Jack.

Chapter Twenty-Five

The crowd of guests stretched all the way down to the barn. Charlotte looked over the sea of faces, which were all now turned towards Rhona. They were the down-to-earth honest faces of good country people. Some of the faces belonged to her dearest friends. From the numbers attending, Charlotte guessed that Ben's estimate of half the county was, if anything, on the low side. Charlotte looked at her daughter. She stood there poised and relaxed. The uncertainty of the last few days had gone. It its place was a quiet confidence.

"I think maybe she got off lightly," thought Charlotte.

The evening had been a huge success. The tables groaning with food had for the most part been cleared and the well-fed and -watered guests were now having a short respite before making their way down towards the barn where a wooden floor had been set out for the dancing which was to come later. For the moment the guests, drinks in hand, were clamouring for a speech.

"I am not going to make a speech," said Rhona. "On a beautiful moonlit night like this, with dancing to come and particularly the promise of an eightsome reel demonstration, this is neither the time nor the place for speeches."

"Speech! Speech!" they all cried.

"Well, just a few, a very few, words then."

"Stand on the table, Rhona, where we can all see you," called a voice from the rear.

There was a cheer when Angus put his hands round her waist and easily lifted her on to the small table in front of her.

"Well, after a full-grown steer, you have to be lightweight, Rhona," called Sam McIver.

When the buzz died down she continued.

"As you know, our very dear visitors from Scotland, who have been such a joy to our community this past week, will, sadly, be leaving us tomorrow. I want to thank them for their visit. We have all thoroughly enjoyed having you and we hope you will return real soon. My friends will you join me in a toast to our dear friends. May they have a safe and pleasant journey home, the best of fortune in the future, and may they all come back to see us one day."

There was a loud cheer and everyone drank their health and slapped them on the back. The Scottish Young Farmers were universally popular.

"You do the honours, Angus," said Dougie Graham.

"Why me?"

"Because you are the biggest and the best-known and you can talk the hind legs off a donkey, anyway."

"Thanks like hell. Oh, all right."

Angus stepped forward.

"Up on the table, Angus!" some one called.

Angus climbed up on the table, beside Rhona.

"I rather think you just want to know whether we do or whether we don't," said Angus. "Well, I'll let you in to a secret. The answer is sometimes we do and sometimes we don't. Tonight I am the soul of propriety. That is why I am up on this table."

"Ah just knew I was gonna be outa luck tonight," said Mary Alice in a loud voice, and a great roar of laughter ran through the assembled guests.

"What can I say?" began Angus. "We were all looking forward to this visit with more than just a little trepidation. Well, the fame of Texas goes a long way before it, and rightly so. When I stood on the verandah one night and saw the moon rise behind the lone pine, it was the most beautiful spectacular sight I have ever seen. It is a picture I shall carry with me for a long time. I knew then beyond any doubt that Texas is the greatest. We were expecting quite something from our visit and we got that and so much more. What we hadn't reckoned with was the hospitality and the warmth of the welcome. We've had a lot of discussion today about whose host is the best. Of course, my hosts were the warmest and most hospitable. Hospitality doesn't come better than on Lone Pine Ranch. The trouble is that I can't seem to convince the others. They all hold the same opinion about their hosts. Anyway, we shall be arguing about that for some time to come.

"We have all learned so much. That at times has not been a wholly easy process. You may have noticed that Dougie Graham has not been sitting down much tonight. Well, Dougie is sporting a new tartan. It is mainly purple, red and black and blue. You can see it cover his rear end, and that is when he is not wearing his kilt. I reckon the score is Texas bucking bronco one, Dougie Graham nil."

The laughter drowned out Angus at that point.

"I'm going to stop here. I tend to get quite emotional when I think just how kind you have all been and I don't want to burst into tears standing up here. From all of us and from the bottom of our hearts, thank you all. We love you dearly."

"I have one last and personal thanks to give. It is to Charlotte, who has been so kind and understanding and just plain lovely. I think she is a great lady, and the best mentor I could possibly have had. Rhona, this for me has been a week to end all weeks and it is all due to you. I admire you greatly. More than ever, I think you are just hell on wheels. I can't find words to thank you."

Angus enveloped her in a big bear hug, kissed her on both cheeks and stepped down from the table.

Rhona brought her emotions under control while the guests all cheered.

"This visit on its own would be quite sufficient reason for celebration at any time, but it so happens that I have another, a very special reason for asking you all here tonight," continued Rhona, when the noise had died down. There was a buzz of interest.

"Tonight, my friends, I am very happy and very proud and it gives me the greatest pleasure to announce that my partner on this ranch, my dear, dear Mom, is to stand for Mayor for the county of San Miguel. My friends, another toast - to Charlotte!"

There was a stunned silence and then an almighty cheer. A surge of gratitude flowed through Charlotte and she loved her daughter more than ever.

"What great timing - she has a lot of her father in her. I am more proud of her now than I ever have been, and that says a lot."

Her eyes grew moist. The company crowded round her. They kissed her and hugged her. It seemed there wasn't a single person who didn't think it a great idea.

Charlotte squeezed Rhona's hand.

"Thank you. I'm very grateful. Just how grateful I shall tell you later? In the meantime, will you hold the fort? I need a little time on my own."

"Sure, Mom. I understand. You go ahead," Rhona whispered, and then she called out to the waiting crowd.

"All, right folks - charge up your glasses and on with the dance."

They all trooped down by the barn. After the turmoil of congratulations, Charlotte took the chance to steal away.

"I think I need to talk with my special friend."

She sat in the shade of the fig tree and was at peace with herself. "Oh Tom," she whispered, "I feel that you are happy with the way things have gone. She was in love with him, but it was not to be. She liked his independent nature and being his own man. In other circumstances, he would have been ideal for her. None of us guessed he was married, but neither did he ever intend to mislead us. Maybe she got off lightly, but we must give time and space for her to be herself too. I think it is time she went out on her own. She is too serious at times. Well, maybe she had reason to be serious. It was a big responsibility for someone so young."

A smile played round the corners of her mouth.

"Tom, I think she is a very fine person. She had a disappointment and she rose above it superbly. I have no worries on her behalf. I hope she finds a good man, one who is his own man too. Oh, Tom, I am content and I sense you are too."

Ben appeared through the archway.

"Mary Alice sent me to see if you are all right. I thought I should find you here. You are all right?"

"Yes, Ben, I am just fine."

"Good. That was one hell of a speech Rhona came up with. I hope it didn't upset you."

"Not at all. Who told her?"

"I did. I talked it over with her before I ever asked you. She thought it was a great deal. She was afraid that you might turn it down because of her. There was no way she was going to have that."

"I'm very proud of her."

"You have every reason to be."

Chapter Twenty-Six

Ben fidgeted and rolled his hat in his hands. His iron-gray hair framed his face and there was a worried, uncertain look about him. It was as though he were trying to make a momentous decision. Charlotte had known him for many years, but had never seen him like this.

"Ben, what's the matter?"

There was a deep sigh.

"You know about Rhona?"

"About Rhona?"

"Yes. You've figured it out."

She nodded silently.

"When?"

"Three days ago. How do you come to know?"

"I've known since she was six months old."

"Does anyone else know?"

"No! I guess I had better tell you."

"Yes."

"Yes, I guess the time has come. I wasn't supposed to tell you till Rhona was twenty-one, but we hadn't reckoned with the arrival of Angus, and, besides, you know now anyway. I think Tom would want me to tell you now. You see Tom pretty well knew from the start that he wasn't the father of Rhona. By the time she was four months old he was certain. What was he to do about that? Tom agonised over that. It just about tore him apart. Above all, he wanted to protect you and to protect Rhona.

"I admired Tom Benson more than any other man I knew. He was the most honourable man I've ever met. I don't think he could have done any one a bad turn ever and where his own family were concerned, he would willingly have laid down his life for any of you. He called me one morning and asked me to meet him out on the range. We spent the morning ostensibly looking at cattle, but I don't recall seeing a single cow that morning.

"He told me the story of your trip to Scotland. He made me swear never to reveal even one word of what he told me that morning and I never have, not to Mary Alice, not to any one. If you get the trust of

some one like Tom Benson, you honour it for all time. He told me
everything, about you, about Hector, about the voyage of discovery
which you and he made through Scotland and after that too. We
talked all morning about what he was going to do.

"He had a major dilemma on his hands. None of what had
happened was really of his doing, but he wasn't the kind of man to
walk away from anything. We talked all morning. We considered a
young man embarking on his career. Were we depriving him? He
already had a son. He was keen to follow his career. There was you,
Charlotte, and the rest of the family. You all adored Rhona and,
above all, there was Rhona. What was best for her? I suggested we
leave things be for a few years and he said that was the conclusion he
had come to, but he wanted to be sure he was not acting from selfish
reasons. You see he adored that little girl. He made me promise that I
would be his judge and jury. I was to keep my eye on how he was
bringing up Rhona and we met once a year to see if we should
change tack. Of course, we never did. I know it was for the best then
and I know it is for the best today. He made discreet enquiries about
Hector and how life was treating him. He has had more than his share
of tragedy in his life and he has risen above it all. We came to the
conclusion that he had enough complications in his life for the
present. Maybe things will change for him. I sure as Hell hope so."

"And I hope so too, Ben. I sincerely hope so."

"How did you figure it out, Charlotte?"

"I knew from the moment I saw Angus just who he was. It was one
of the most traumatic episodes in my life. I almost fainted on the
spot. He was just so like his father. I kept telling myself it wasn't
real. Things like that don't happen in real life, but it had. It was real.
There was no doubting it."

"Yes, life is quite often stranger than fiction, but go on."

"I got over the initial shock quite well, but there was just something
else bothering me. I couldn't put it into context. But it was always
there, just on the edge of consciousness."

"You see, Ben, it was the time that had completely deluded me.
You would think that a woman's instinct would have told her, but it
didn't, and then one night Angus was telling us the story of Alan nan
Sop. Alan is his ancestor, and legend has it that his mother was under
the spell of a witch and had to carry the child she was expecting for
eighteen months. As Angus said, that it pure legend, but it is a fact

Printed in the United Kingdom
by Lightning Source UK Ltd.
101891UKS00001B/148-156

that Maclean wives often carry their children for a bit longer than is customary and that trait is passed down the male line.

"Ben, I knew in that instant what had been bothering me. It all crystalised in that instant. I knew that Rhona was Hector's daughter. I knew that she and Angus were of the same blood. Ben, what a week this has been. I don't know how I have kept my sanity."

"Charlotte, it isn't an expression I ever use in front of a lady and forgive me for using it now, but, Honey, your ass sure has been in the blender this week. "

Charlotte smiled. This was most unexpected coming from Ben. She was surprised that he even knew the expression far less used it.

"Have you heard anything of Hector over the years?"

"Nothing till this week. Angus is a great talker and so open and innocent with it. Like most Highlanders, he is a great storyteller. He has been telling us in the course of conversation what Hector has been doing and how he fared. I couldn't bring myself to ask, but Rhona seemed to take quite an interest in him. I longed to know and I blessed her whenever she would ask. Ben, you would actually think there was some instinct at work there."

"Maybe there was, Charlotte. We don't know everything about everything. She fell in love with him, didn't she?"

Charlotte nodded.

"She didn't know he was married. It was just one of those things. It was all there in the briefing notes, but Rhona didn't get around to reading them. He never thought of mentioning the fact right away and he was so engrossed with learning about ranching, it took up every conversation."

"Yes, that figures. How did she find out he was married?"

"Again, it was just during conversation. Angus was telling us about how devastated Hector was when his wife died. He mentioned then that his two sons did more to get him on his feet than anything else."

"That was a good way for her to find out. It solves that particular problem, but there remains the other one."

"Yes, Ben, there remains the other one."

"Any ideas?"

"No, my instinct is to let it be for the present."

"That is good thinking. There is no need to rush into anything."

"I think, though, she should get away for a spell. I have talked it over with Connie. I'm pretty sure she will take off for Dallas very soon for a short spell and then she is going to Scotland for the christening of Morag and Angus's daughter. They have asked Rhona to be their little girl's Godmother. She is thrilled at that prospect."

"Yes and well she might be. God, Charlotte, I've just thought - that little girl will be Rhona's niece. You know, we don't know what forces are at work behind the scenes. You could never figure that one out. In life, truth is often stranger than fiction."

"Yes, I've thought so myself many times in the past few days."

"Will she meet her natural father?"

"Almost certainly."

"What do you think will happen then?"

"Ben, I've no idea. There is no way you could foretell what will happen."

"No, I agree. Do you think we should prepare her in any way?"

"I don't know, Ben. I think we should give it a bit more thought. My instincts say no. Something tells me to leave things be for the present. You know, it was Hector who said to me once, 'Rely on your instincts, Charlotte. It is all there.' And do you know, I've always tended to do just that."

"And he was right. I think you should do just that. Meantime, a spell away from the ranch won't harm her any."

"Yes, I think that will do her good. That will give her the chance to meet some one   else."

"Yes, I hope that happens soon, quite soon. You know, Charlotte, he's one hell of a guy. In other circumstances, he would have been ideal for her."

"Yes, Ben, I thought that too, and thank you very much for telling me. It means a great deal to me, Ben. You've always taken such an interest in Rhona's well being. Now I know why."

"I would have done that, anyway, even without the added interest. You know, we are not prying into your affairs Charlotte, but Mary Alice and I often discuss Rhona. We both think she is a wonderful person. How else could she be, considering the stock she springs from, and match-make as we may, we can't see any one that would be suitable for her."

"Nor me, Ben."

She saw again the nubile handsome couple walking in the moonlight and she remembered the upturned eager face of her daughter.

"The Maclean men seem destined to play havoc with our lives," she thought.

"I think it is time we went back down to the barn."

She slipped her arm through his. They paused on the edge of the verandah. The range spread out before them. In the moonlight it looked somehow mysterious.

"It is very beautiful country this, Ben," she said. "Ideal country for young people to start out. It is up to our generation to make sure it stays that way to let the next generation have their chance."

"Hmm. You know, Charlotte, you are one hell of a fine woman."

She was lying back on her pillow savouring again the events of that momentous day, when the door opened and Rhona stole into her room and sat down on her bed. It was the first time she had ever done this.

"I just came to thank you, Mom. I just want to thank you for being so understanding."

"My pleasure and thank you. You have done very well, Rhona. I am proud of you, very very proud."

"Thanks Mom. That means a lot to me."

"By the way, I was on the phone to your Aunt Connie yesterday, to invite her to our party. She just couldn't make it. She says she is sick as a parrot at missing the party. She is all tied up in one of her schemes. She wonders if you could come to Dallas to help her out. I told her you were busy with your visitors, but I said you would call her back Sunday. Maybe you could do that."

"I can't go Mom. I'd love to, but I can't."

"Why not?"

"I can't leave you at this time. You can't run the ranch and canvass for the election for Mayor at the same time. No, Mom, I can't do it, much as I would like to."

"Don't give the election for Mayor a second thought. Ben and his cronies have decided it is to be me, and me it will be, come hell or high water. I shall not be doing much canvassing. In fact, Ben says that I won't need to canvass. No one in this county is crazy enough to waste time standing against me. After tonight, I think he may be right. As for the ranch, well, Mike and Ben are always there if I need them, and I think young Tom wants to take a bigger part in the running of the ranch. Maybe it is time to let him cut his teeth."

"Are you sure, Mom?"

"Certain."

"Well, in that case I'll phone Aunt Connie on Sunday. Come to think of it, I do need a break. I can't stay too long. There is Scotland later on, you know, but, yeah, a little while will do me good."

"Yes there is Scotland later on," thought Charlotte, when Rhona had left her, and that will bring with it problems too. Hector will certainly be there and she will meet him. I wonder if he will deduce that she is his offspring. The possibility is always there. What we are to do about that I do not yet know. We'll find the answer in due course."

"Life is not about avoiding problems. That is one thing that I have learned. I think that real life satisfaction comes from developing the qualities and the experience to solve them. And then, I have always you to turn to, Tom; I have always you, my lover."

End